Holiday Homecomings-

Tales to Warm The Heart

Volume Two

‡‡‡

A Collection

By,
B.K. Ritter

For Emma and Dale...

Life truly is what you make it...

✝✝✝

Dear Reader,
"I'll be home for Christmas, if only in my dreams..."
"Oh, there's no place like home for the holidays..."
Those old songs can bring a smile to your face and a sigh to your heart.
Because they make you yearn for home. Your home.
The wreath on the front door.
The steamy kitchen window, lit from within.
The menorah on the living room mantle.
The smell of good cooking wafting out to the sidewalk leading to the house.
The people inside, waiting for you.
You know your way there. You always have. You always will.
Time to head home.

When you get there, find a little time to put your feet up, put on an old Bing Crosby Christmas record, and let the welcoming warmth of home wrap itself around you. Then, take the time to lose yourself in a good book...like this one!
Happy Holidays from my home to yours!
‡‡‡

I would love to hear from you... please contact me at
bkritterbooks@gmail.com

Contents

I don't believe in fate. I do believe in meddling angels, acts of God and the whimsy of a Universe we don't fully understand.   And I certainly never discount a little bit of well-intentioned magic. Especially during the holidays...

The Coat

To the saints of St. Luke's Episcopal Church in Gresham, Oregon... my family of choice...

The parking lot was crammed. Anna closed her eyes and sighed heavily as she turned off the engine and listened to the rain pound on the roof of the car. Rooting around in the back seat, she grabbed the "emergency" umbrella and stepped out into what could only be described as a deluge, even for Seattle. Dragging a wet cart from the queue while trying to hold the umbrella upright, Anna managed to muscle her way into the humid warmth of the store. Shaking out the umbrella, she apologized to the guy stalking past her, scowling at her as she shot droplets of rain onto his suit pants. The scowl turned to a glare and he muttered something derogatory, which Anna chose not to take personally.

After all, it was the day before Thanksgiving. His mood had to be excused, right? Last minute grocery shopping for Thanksgiving dinner was enough to put anyone in *anything* but a festive mood. Add the torrential rains and seemingly perpetual darkness, and you had the perfect recipe for the early arrival of Scrooge in a business suit, complete with a heartfelt "Bah, humbug." Anna sighed again, knowing that was not even close to what the guy had said to her. She stuffed her reusable grocery bags into the bottom of the cart and squared her shoulders, prepared to brave the hordes battling for the last of the turkeys.

The produce department spread out before her as she entered the store. But, before she headed for the cranberries and onions, she steered the cart toward the clearance racks stuck off to the side by the clothing departments. You had to love stores with "one stop" shopping, she thought. Everything from apples to screwdrivers, from ottomans to underwear. All under one roof. And, as predictable as sunrise, right next to the entrance was rack after rack of discounted clothing from the season past, pulling her toward it like a Siren's song. Anna loved a bargain.

The racks were crowded and she was soon engulfed in sweaters and t-shirts and last season's jeans. As she muscled her way through the makeshift aisle, an ugly winter coat shifted off its hanger and fell into her cart. Anna pulled it out and held it up. Shiny material, a crazy striped pattern of purple and muddy brown, it had fake purple fur around the hood and sleeves. "Wow," she said out loud. "This is some

9

coat." She shook her head and shoved it back on the rack and turned to look through the sweaters.

When she turned back, the coat was back in the cart. Anna's brow furrowed. Hmmm. Holding up the coat, she searched for the price tag. It was marked down so many times it was almost free. Turning it, she tilted her head and squinted. It would fit Jocelyn. Maybe her daughter could use it for outdoor chores or for trips to school on the bus. It really was too good a deal to pass up. So, she dropped it back into the cart and headed for produce.

"No way, Mom!" her daughter made gagging noises and poked a finger into her mouth when Anna showed her the coat. "You have got to be kidding me! I wouldn't be caught dead in that rag! And no one else would either! That's the ugliest thing I've ever seen in my life!"

Anna held up the coat and tried to brush the purple fur collar, as if that would make it look more attractive. She loved this daughter of hers, her only child. But there were times when her over-the-top reactions made Anna just a little bit crazy. "But, Jocelyn," she said in a soothing voice with just a hint of pleading, "couldn't you wear it on the bus? You know how you like to wear old clothes so you don't get your good clothes dirty. Or maybe you could just use it to do the yard chores. It's thick and warm. Surely..."

Her 17-year-old drama queen put her hands on her hips and sneered. "Absolutely not! Look at that thing! It's hideous! I wouldn't be able to show my face in town ever again if someone saw me in that thing!" Jocelyn flicked at hand at the shiny fabric. "You should give it to the homeless shelter. Maybe someone there is desperate enough to want it." Looking at the coat, she shook her head. "But probably not." She flounced out of the room, still shaking her head, leaving Anna holding the ugly coat.

Thanksgiving Day came and went in a flurry of blowing leaves, football scores, and delicious smells coming from the kitchen. Anna bustled around the kitchen, then sat down to the table with her daughter and an elderly neighbor from down the street. She watched as her daughter entertained Mrs. Entemann with stories about school and friends.

Anna's heart swelled. Jocelyn was counted as her absolute best blessing. Her gaze rested on the framed photo of her husband, Greg, gone so many years now. She missed him every day. Theirs had been a good, solid marriage, a bond of friendship and love. They had wanted more children, but Jocelyn was their one and only. They had formed a warm circle of three, and that had been enough. Anna was the nurturer, the baker, the healer of boo-boos. Greg was the fixer of all things and the teller of silly jokes. Jocelyn rooted and grew in her parents' absolute love and caring.

When Greg died so unexpectedly, Anna and Jocelyn had closed ranks, leaning on each other in their grief. Losing Greg had forged a close, loving relationship that tied them together with a bond impossible to break. But always something felt a little uneven in their family of two. There seemed to be extra love to give away. They became great givers of time and energy to those in need. That seemed to fill the gap. Almost.

They had each other. But even that was changing. This June, Jocelyn would graduate from high school and move on to college. Anna's heart beat a little faster at that. She was thrilled by her daughter's excitement and all the possibilities of life opening up for Jocelyn. But oh, how she was going to miss her.

"Mom, are you OK?" Jocelyn's voice snapped her out of her reverie and she turned to find both her daughter and her neighbor peering questioningly at her. "You were sighing so hard I thought you were going to blow out the candles."

Mrs. Entemann chuckled. "Oh, I think your mom was just having a brisk walk down Memory Lane," she said and her eyes twinkled. "Been jogging down that path a few times myself." She looked at Anna with understanding. "It kind of takes your breath away, doesn't it, Anna?"

"Oh, brother," Jocelyn said as she pushed away from the table. "Memory Lane. She's probably thinking about the time I was being 'helpful' and dropped the bowl of mashed potatoes onto Dad's lap." She turned to Mrs. Entemann. "He jumped up, howling, scaring Mom so bad she dropped the champagne. The cork popped as the bottle shattered, hitting Uncle Ed in the back of the head, and he darn near sliced his hand off as he was carving the turkey!" She shook her head as they all dissolved into gales of laughter. "Good times," she said. Anna couldn't agree more.

On Sunday morning, with things back to some semblance of normal, she went into the laundry room to collect the bags she'd packed with canned food and toiletries. Their church would take the items to the soup kitchen, which had a food pantry. Flipping on the light, she grabbed the first bag, then stopped with a puzzled frown. There, on top of one of the bags, neatly folded, lay the coat.

"Honey, I think the shelter only wants food items," she said as her daughter came in to help.

"What are you talking about?" Jocelyn asked.

"The coat," Anna said. "I don't know if they can accept clothing items.

Jocelyn looked at the coat like it had fleas. "I didn't put that there," she said with a sniff. "I wouldn't touch that thing!" She grabbed a bag of food and started past her mother. "But," she said on her way out to the garage, "you should add it to the baskets. It is a warm coat. I bet they can find someone to use it."

Anna looked at the coat, shrugged, and hoisted the bag to take it out to the car.

In the church parking lot, as they were taking the bags out of the car, the coat fell out and landed under the back tire. Anna's arms were full, so she just slammed the car door and hurried on. She'd come back for the coat after she dropped the first load off. As soon as she entered the church, she was enveloped by her gregarious, engaging church family. Arms reached out to take the bags and then to hug Anna. Jocelyn was further in front, with friends from school. The coat was immediately forgotten.

About midway through the service, Anna sat back and smiled as she watched church members bring forward basket after basket of donated goods toward the altar for the pastor to bless. She loved this part. Helping others was so important to her, and it was heartening to see that so many others contributed as well. The food and toiletry items would go a long way, she thought, to… the thought evaporated in her head as her mouth gaped open and she goggled. For there, in one of the baskets, on top of a pile of canned goods, lay the coat in all its ugly glory. It was impossible to miss.

"Did you…" Anna turned to her daughter, but stopped midsentence. She knew that Jocelyn had been ahead of her when the coat had fallen out of the bag. And she knew Jocelyn hadn't gone back to the car. How the coat had gotten into that basket was a mystery. The silly thing seemed to have legs instead of arms.

Anna shook her head. "Good-bye, you weird coat," she whispered. Jocelyn snickered and added, "and *good riddance.*"

The new year blew in and then suddenly, it was June, then September. Anna watched her daughter drive off to the University of Washington in her second-hand Subaru. She spent a couple of days moping around in her pajamas, the host of her own pity party. She used every Kleenex in the house, aching for Jocelyn. Mrs. Entemann stopped by on the third day, gave Anna a hug and a stern talking-to. Anna heaved a last heavy sigh, picked herself up, took a long shower, and got on with the business of life.

The next couple of months flew by. The next thing Anna knew, another holiday season was upon them. Jocelyn was out of school for the holiday break, and Anna was busy trying to get to know this new person who inhabited her daughter's body. A restless energy radiated from her daughter, as an adult maturity wrestled with the teenage craziness Anna knew so well. Anna knew it was coming. She'd been warned. But as much as she'd tried to prepare, Jocelyn's first week home was a tornado of tangled emotions and frustrated female histrionics.

Jocelyn had wandered into the kitchen complaining about the water temperature in the shower. That had segued into a whining dissertation that there wasn't the kind of yogurt she liked in the fridge and the coffee was too weak. Anna wanted to scream. She turned, yanked open the refrigerator door, and pulled out a big hunk of Swiss. Slamming it on the counter, she looked at her daughter and said,

"Want some cheese to go with that whine? What in God's name is the matter with you these days?"

"What's the matter with *me?* What's the matter with *you?*" Jocelyn was almost screeching. "You treat me like a little kid, expect me to do whatever you want, just like it was before!"

"I don't treat you like a little kid, but I am having a hard time seeing the adult you've supposedly become. Right now, all I see is a spoiled brat who thinks that everything is her way or the highway!" Anna threw her arm out and encompassed the room. "Nothing is right around here for you- there's something wrong with everything!" Anna's voice vibrated with frustration. "I was so looking forward to seeing you- but I hardly even *know* you anymore!"

"I hardly know you either!" Jocelyn slammed her coffee cup down on the counter, and coffee sloshed over the side. The puddle spread and they both just stared at it. The dark stain seemed a fitting statement to the current state of their lives together.

Because there it was. Out in the open. Both of them were changing. Both were ready for new things, new people. Anna realized that she was growing and changing just as much as Jocelyn. Who was she now? What did she want? She had given everything she had to her daughter. And she'd obviously done a good job. Jocelyn was bright and smart and strong, ready to fly. She didn't need Anna anymore.

But Anna was still a nurturer at heart. She had so much love to give. And Jocelyn needed things Anna couldn't give her. That uneven place they'd tried so hard to fix and forget sat before them. The need for something more. It tilted them a little bit off balance.

Anna stared at her daughter. "A lot is different for you now, I get it. But a lot is different for me, too." She blew out a breath, her anger evaporating, replaced by a thin sheen of discontent. "I've been anticipating this visit so much, that I probably put a Polyanna spin on it."

Jocelyn looked at her mother with a puzzled frown. "What is a Polyanna?" she asked.

Anna laughed, a short bark. "Obviously, I was remiss in the stories I told you as a child," she said. Then she looked at her daughter and said, "OK, young woman-of-the-world, let's talk."

Jocelyn opened her mouth, retort at the ready. Then she shut it again. She looked at Anna and Anna could feel the air clear between them. Then Jocelyn gave her a saucy look, opened the drawer and took out a knife. "Okay," she said, slamming the drawer shut. "But wait until I get a piece of this delicious cheese!" Her daughter smiled as she sliced and Anna rolled her eyes, smiling too. Everything was going to be alright.

A good old heart-to-heart led to a comfortable truce. Each was willing to acknowledge that the changes in their lives had enriched them, but it also made them a bit melancholy. It was great to be moving on to new things, but it came with an ache for the past. Change came with a few strings attached. They agreed to disagree on some things, and to make adjustments on others that they could both live with.

They discussed what they wanted to do with this holiday time to make it special. Together they decided to do some volunteering with some other church members at a local soup kitchen. It had worked in the past. Helping others brought back that sense of balance, to the greatest extent possible.

Each day, they went and prepared, then helped serve meals. Side by side, they quietly ladled helpings of soup and bread to equally quiet individuals and families. Every day, it seemed, the increasingly cold weather brought more and more people in for warmth and sustenance. The good work of the soup kitchen helped. But there was so much need. So many people without a home.

They'd been there about a week, when Jocelyn stopped, holding a ladle of stew in mid-air. Anna turned to see her daughter staring slack-jawed into the dining room.

"I don't believe it," Jocelyn said in an odd voice. "It can't be."

Anna followed her daughter's gaze. "What are you talking about?" She looked at Jocelyn, who had gone a little pale. "Honey, are you OK?"

Still staring out into the room, Jocelyn said, "Mom. It's the coat."

"What?" Anna said. "What coat?"

"THE coat," Jocelyn said, her voice tinged with awe. "That ugly, stupid coat. It's back."

Jocelyn handed Anna the ladle she'd been holding and headed out into the dining room. Anna grabbed the ladle before it fell, and tried to follow her daughter's path with her eyes. A man holding a bowl looked at Anna with a patient question in his eyes and Anna smiled weakly and spooned the stew into the bowl, apologizing for her daughter. "Sorry. She just saw...someone she knew." Anna looked out into the dining room and saw her daughter talking with a young woman about her age. Jocelyn was right. It was the same coat she'd given away last Christmas. The coat hung from the girl's thin shoulders, glinting strangely in the overhead fluorescent lights, a beacon drawing Anna's attention. The girl looked tired, wet and cold, yet she laughed lightly when Jocelyn said something and pointed to her coat. The sound carried all the way through the crowd to Anna's ears. And somehow went straight to her heart.

"Excuse me," Anna said to another volunteer. She untied her apron and pulled it over her head, her eyes never leaving the girl in the coat. "Could you take over for me for a few minutes? There's something... no, there's someone I have to meet." The woman took her apron with a nod and smile. The sea of people parted as Anna moved toward the two girls. Jocelyn turned and smiled at her mother. "Mom," she said with that same awe in her voice, "this is Abigail. Abigail, this is my mom, Anna." She looked at Anna, then back at Abigail, then down at the coat. "I was just telling Abigail about the coat. And she was telling me..." Jocelyn shook her head. "Well, it appears that the coat is still up to its old tricks."

"I'm serious," Abigail said, with a steaming mug of cocoa in her hands. "I kept putting it back, thinking that there was someone else that needed it more." She smoothed her hand down the sleeve, which was stained and had a long, jagged tear. "But every time I put it back in the pile at the shelter store, it ended up back in my backpack after I left. It's like the thing had a mind of its own. Too weird. " She shrugged. "I finally just figured that someone from the shelter really felt I should have it." She sighed. "It's not much to look at, but it's warm and repels water really well." She looked shyly at Anna. "I've really appreciated having it. Thank you for donating it."

Anna and Jocelyn looked at each other in a warm moment of awareness. The crazy coat was back in their lives. From the moment it fell into Anna's basket at the store to the moment it's ugly sheen had caught Jocelyn's eye, it seemed that the coat had a mission. And not just to keep a young girl warm.

Anna looked at Abigail. Abigail's story was simple and heartbreaking- selfish, mean-spirited parents caught up in a web of alcohol and drug abuse. When Abigail found herself on the verge of succumbing to the same, she'd given her parents an ultimatum. A choice. Her parents chose, alright. They kicked her out of the house. Abigail moved around, did odd jobs for money, and came to shelters for safety when she needed it. Hers was a story of determination and survival.

She'd come to this area because she'd heard there was an organization that might be able to help her find work and get back to school. It was her first time in this soup kitchen. Anna looked at Jocelyn, who nodded decisively at the unspoken question. In that instant, their slightly uneven life became perfectly balanced.

This might have been Abigail's first time at this shelter. But, if Anna had anything to say about it, it would be her last.

It was two days before Christmas. Down the hall, two female voices started bickering, their voices rising. Anna held her breath, then started down the hall, prepared to referee. Suddenly, just as quickly as it started, the bickering stopped and rollicking laughter took its place. Anna stopped and smiled. There was nothing like the sound of a daughter laughing.

Unless it was two.

"Come on, girls, let's get going!" Anna finished pulling on her gloves and continued down the hall. "That tree isn't going to cut itself!" And she laughed as two almost-adult girls came tumbling out of their room, pulling on their boots. They scrambled for the closet, pulling out hats and gloves, then yanking coats off the hanger.

"Oh, God, you're not going to wear that thing, are you?" Jocelyn rolled her eyes and made the gagging motion as Abigail shoved her arms into the sleeves of the ugly coat.

"Well, it's my coat," she said as she zipped it up.

"Not for long," Anna's heard her daughter mutter as she zipped up her own coat and headed for the garage. "There's a match with that coat's name on it!" Then she sped up and yanked the garage door open, shouting, "I'm driving!"

Abigail stopped and almost pouted. Just like any younger sister. Then she yelled, "OK, but I call 'shotgun!'" Anna gladly climbed into the back seat, and off they went to the tree farm. They picked out the biggest tree they could find.

Under that tree on Christmas Day was a big box with a new coat for Abigail.

It was a frigid February day and Anna opened the hall closet to get her gloves. And there it was. The coat. It hung there, as it had since Christmas, always front and center whenever anyone opened the closet. No matter how far back Jocelyn shoved it, it always seemed to be the first thing they saw when they opened the closet door. Jocelyn threated daily to take the horrid old thing out and burn it in the barbeque pit. And yet, here it hung, tattered and dirty, with a rip on the sleeve and the ugly purple fur matted and thin. Even Jocelyn couldn't seem to strike the match.

Anna smiled and ran her hand down the sleeve, seeing Abigail as she'd been at the homeless shelter that day, and knowing how different she looked now. The adoption was in motion. Abigail's parents had signed away their parental rights. Abigail spent exactly one minute mourning over their desertion. Then she wiped her eyes, blew her nose and hugged Anna. Hard. Anna was now her mother. Jocelyn was her sister. And Anna would make sure she never had cause to doubt that.

Anna grabbed her gloves. Before she closed the closet door, she took the coat and hung it up in the far back of the closet. As she closed the door, she could have sworn she heard a rustling noise. She opened the closet door, and there it was, front and center again. A constant reminder of the answer to a prayer Anna never even realized she'd uttered. She didn't bother anymore trying to understand. She just accepted the ugly, tattered coat for what it was. The miracle that had brought another daughter into her waiting heart.

Crazy coat.

The end of the war in Iraq brought a flood of soldiers home to waiting family and friends, just in time for the holidays.

But many dedicated military personnel were left behind. They are still waiting to come home...

Soldier's Homecoming

To those who Serve...

Amy moved closer to the computer screen, reading the message again, even though she knew it by heart.
> *Have received medical release*
> *and military clearance for*
> *departure. Gotta hurry so I can*
> *make the transport.*
> *Home tomorrow. xxoo*

Home tomorrow. David was coming home. Finally.

"Mom?" Jonathan, her oldest son, peered over her shoulder at the screen. "Is that from Dad?"
Amy swiped the tear from her cheek and turned to give her 8-year-old a squeeze. She smiled at him to remove the worried look from his eyes. "Yes, it's from Dad, Nosey Rosey." She poked him in the ribs before

letting him go, making him jump and laugh. "By this time tomorrow, he will be home with us."

She grinned, then grew serious. "So, young man, you and Private Sean better get in the bath and get those rooms in order. You know what happens when you don't pass Daddy's inspection!"

She laughed as Jonathan squealed and pulled away from her. "No! Not the upside-down tummy tickle! That always makes Sean pee his pants!" Jonathan ran out the door yelling for his brother. "Sean! Where are you? We've got to get our rooms cleaned up! Dad is coming home for inspection!" Feet pounded down the hallway as Jonathan and his brother collided into each other.

"Oh no!" Sean yelled. "Inspection!" His voice squeaked in mock six-year-old horror. "If Daddy saw my room right now, I would be in big trouble! I'd better stop drinking water right now!" The boys' voices disappeared down the hall. "And wear extra underwear tomorrow!" More squealing and laughing ensued as the boys headed for their rooms, determined to have them in perfect shape when their father got home.

They were so excited, so *relieved.* The weeks had crawled by, the drone of everyday living punctuated with the pins and needles of worry and anxiety. Ever since the call had come with news of David's injury, the direction of their lives had changed. On the surface, everything seemed normal. Carpools, soccer games, homework, supper, baths, prayers before bed. But beneath the normal was a new focus. Every movement, every event, every meal brought them one moment closer to the day when David would come home. So they could see for themselves that he was truly okay.

Living with a soldier was not easy. Commitment to the soldier meant commitment to the military and all that it entailed. When the soldier was at home there were frequent transfers, causing the family to be uprooted and replanted. Amy learned that it wasn't worth unpacking all the boxes. They would just need to be repacked. And there were no gardens, no tree houses, no pets. It was best to keep it simple. Be ready to go at any time.

Deployment was a whole different kind of uprooting. Saying goodbye the first time as a new wife was difficult enough. Saying goodbye this last time with two young children clinging to her was devastating. Routine was essential, and Amy had worked hard to create the most normal family life for the boys as she could. She tried to make their family just the same as any other family. But the difference in living with a soldier was that everything was about *today*. During deployment, no one planned for the future, no one talked about tomorrow or next week or next year. Other families might be dreaming about that trip to Disneyland or buying that bigger house, the one with the playhouse out back. Amy didn't do that. She had her hands full just planning on getting through the day.

When the call came, David had just six months left to his deployment. Each day marked off the calendar was one day closer to having him with them again. They had even begun to tentatively say the magic words "when Dad gets home."

Amy always thought she was prepared. In the dark of the night she had planned and rehearsed. But, when she grabbed the phone that Friday afternoon, the deep, kind voice on the phone surprised her. She had been busy baking cupcakes for Sean's bake sale at school. Her hair was up in a high ponytail, she was holding a wooden spoon in her hand and she had chocolate frosting on her t-shirt.

Words came out of the phone, into her ear. Words like "IED," "injured," "left leg," and "facility in Germany." She watched as the words floated around the room like balloons. She couldn't hear them, though. Because all she could hear was the high, thin wail that keened upward from her soul, filling her ears with its screeching terror. Time stopped, and the air around her froze into crystalline shards, like ice on a lake.

Four days later, he was stable enough to call. Amy clutched the phone in her hand, trying to understand what he was saying, trying to hear beyond the words, making sure he was really going to be alright.

"It all happened so fast," David said. His voice was slurred from the pain medication. "One second we were...we were checking out a house on the outskirts of town. Then, Soldier, he..." David stopped and drew a deep breath.

"Soldier? What soldier?" Amy tried to get her husband to focus, to talk more, even though she knew he was exhausted. But she had to hear his voice. It was the only thing keeping her sane.

David grunted, as if she had woken him up. He cleared his throat. "Soldier... he knew. He pulled away, but I kept going... wasn't paying attention to him. If I had been..."

"Oh, David," she said. "you couldn't have known there was a bomb."

"Yeah, but Soldier... he did. That's what he's supposed to do. And he was doing it, Amy. He was trying to tell me. But we were looking for a weapon's cache, and the information had been good." He paused and took a deep breath. "I really thought we were on to something. I was heading for a door that I thought would lead to a cellar..." He stopped talking and there was a crackling sound. What he was telling her was being monitored and someone was interfering with the transmission to keep classified information from being leaked. Even to a wife.

"David? Are you there?"

"... next thing I knew, he crashed into me and knocked me back. We fell into a heap just as the bomb went off." David's voice came back on the line, but his words were slurring again. "He saved my life," her husband said and his voice cracked. "He saved my life... and I don't even know how he is."

"Who? What was his name? Maybe I can find out..." Amy was cut off as David's voice floated over the line.

"Soldier," he said. And then there was silence. Amy called his name, but he had drifted off to sleep again. A nurse came on the line, told her everything was fine, that Captain Pollard was making good progress, that he was a lucky man. Then the call was ended, leaving Amy to think about her husband, the shrapnel in his leg, and the soldier that had kept that shrapnel from piercing his heart.

There is a bond between soldiers that can never be understood by a civilian. There are things that only a soldier can know. What seems unimaginable to a civilian has been written on the psyche of every soldier.   Each one has paid a price. And every other one respects and honors the cost.

Amy Pollard understood that as she stood in the arrivals area of the airport, waiting for her husband. Along the rails, families waved signs and tiny American flags, craning to catch a glimpse of their loved one in the slow line of passengers de-planing. A dozen members of the Patriot Guard stood at quiet attention, with leather vests and long hair tied back in ponytails, tattoos on burly arms and old metal POW bracelets wrapped around thin wrists. Amy knew that another dozen members of this silent, watchful group waited out on the tarmac, saluting as caskets wrapped in American flags were carried off the plane. No American soldier came home alone. There would always be a member of the Patriot Guard to welcome them back to U.S. soil or to lead them to their final resting place.

The atmosphere in the airport was somber for some and jubilant for others. It swirled together in an emotional blend that belongs only to those with loved ones in the military.

David was one of the first off the plane. Amy watched her husband limp down the jetway, leaning heavily on a cane. He stopped, saluting those who had come to welcome the returning soldiers home, shaking hands, even getting a hug from another soldier's mother. She felt the tug of a thousand emotions colliding inside her. Joy. Hope. Dread. David's life would never be the same again. Neither would hers. War changed a family. David's wounds proved that. He was not whole. He had left parts of himself in Afghanistan. Important parts. And she knew her job was to help make him whole again.

She swiped a tear away, squared her shoulders, and squeezed the boys' hands, then let them go to run to their father. A few of the Patriot Guards chuckled as Sean and Jonathan almost knocked their father off his feet, but David managed to right himself, then bent over to engulf his sons in his embrace. He buried his face in their hair, closing his eyes tight. The moment was frozen in time as David absorbed his sons into his weary soul.

Then, taking the boys by the hand, he stood up tall and his gaze locked on Amy. With a determined stride, he led the boys to where she stood and they looked at each other for a long moment. Then Amy opened her arms and welcomed her husband home.

Late that night, she woke to find David's side of the bed empty. But she could see his silhouette in the bedroom window.

"David? Honey? Are you alright?" Her voice was soft and he turned to her. Is something wrong? You've seemed unsettled all afternoon. I know this is a lot to take in, but it seems as if you're a thousand miles away."

"I've had a great day, and I'm so grateful to be home," he said and came to sit on the side of the bed. He ran a hand down her arm. "I've missed you and the boys so much." He smiled in the dark; she could feel it. But then he looked up and away, out the window again. "I'm just having a hard time settling down."

"But there's more," Amy said. She knew her husband well. "Please tell me."

David scratched his head and Amy turned on the bedside table. "You'll probably think I'm silly," he said. "Emotional soldier time. Time to call in the shrink." He sighed. "But I've been thinking about Soldier. I'm worried about him."

Amy nodded. "Soldier? Which soldier?" She frowned. She remembered her husband talking about a soldier when he'd first arrived at the hospital. He'd never said anything again and, frankly, there had been so many other things to think about that Amy had forgotten about it. David had said a soldier had saved his life, throwing himself on David to protect him from the blast.

David stood up and went to the window. "Not which soldier," he said. "Soldier is his name." He

31

turned and looked at Amy. "I know I couldn't tell you much about what I was doing in Afghanistan. But most of the time we were searching for Taliban strongholds, the small out-of-the-way places where they would stash their artillery. Soldier was part of our unit. He was trained to sniff out bombs and IEDs." David ran his hand through his hair again. "Soldier is a dog. I was his handler. We've been together since I arrived in Afghanistan. I know it might sound overly sentimental to you, but that dog was a full member of our platoon. We ate together. We slept together. We took on the Taliban together. He was a professional. And one hell of a comrade."

Amy was confused. "Are you telling me that this dog, this Soldier, is the one you talked about in the hospital? The one you said saved your life?"

David nodded. "We were in this tiny house. There was a door that I thought led to a cellar. We had good quality intel that said there was a heavy cache hidden there. I was hot and heavy to find it and trap the militants that were hiding it. I wasn't paying attention." He shook his head and his voice was rough when he spoke again. "Soldier started whining and pulling away. I couldn't understand what he was doing. He's trained to locate and stand by when he smells explosives. He can usually detect them at a safe distance. But, we had come upon this one so fast, and got too close." He looked at Amy with anguish in his eyes. "Soldier was pulling away, trying to get me to safety. When I didn't respond, he lunged at me, knocking me back flat just as the bomb went off."

"Oh, my God," Amy whispered and covered her heart with her hand.

"He was on top of me when the device exploded. Hill and Gillis were back further and were clear of the main part of the blast." David looked down at his leg. "Soldier took the brunt of the blast. He was in worse shape than I was when we were Medivaced out."

Amy was aghast. "But how is he now? Did he make it? Is he better?"

David shook his head and ran his hand through his hair. "Yeah, he's better. I saw him before I left. But that's the problem, Amy. I left. And he didn't."

Amy sat up in bed. Her husband's tone was serious.

"These dogs are fearless," he continued. "They know their job and they do it every day, no questions asked. They're the perfect combat personnel." He turned back to her. "Yet they're not considered military personnel. They are considered equipment."

Amy frowned again. "Equipment? But then, what happens to them when their tour of duty is over?"

David turned to her, a shadow in the night. "They're not soldiers. They can't retire. They don't have a home to go to. They're considered surplus." He shrugged. "And, as with all Army surplus, ultimately it becomes obsolete." He paused. "Then it's gotten rid of."

Amy was flabbergasted. "He saved your life. Doesn't the Army take that into account?"

He sighed. "I tried. But I was shot down with every suggestion. It's too expensive. So, Soldier stays in Afghanistan. They'll take care of him for awhile. But he's got no future. We're so proud of the fact that we never leave a comrade behind." David's voice grew tired and soft. "I guess that's not really true."

He lay down on the bed next to her and the silence lengthened between them. Both were lost in their own thoughts. Soon his breathing grew deep as exhaustion carried him into sleep. But Amy was awake for many hours. Thinking.

The next several months flew by, a series of jolts and bumps as a military family adjusts to their loved one being home. Amy had been through this once before, when David had been deployed several years earlier.

But, this time was different. David was different. He seemed to have retreated somehow. He couldn't seem to find his place, being out of the combat zone. He was often testy and tense, dismissive or exclusionary. The boys began acting out, picking fights with each other, getting into minor scrapes at school. Amy's nerves were frazzled, trying to referee the boys and cheer David on as he contemplated his future.

You could cut the tension in the house with a knife. Arguments were the rule of the day. Just this morning, Amy had forced David to keep his physical therapy appointment. He had missed the previous three. David had whined about it, then exploded when she wouldn't give in. "What's the use?" he'd howled. In the end, he'd gone, but the car ride there and back was icy. The therapy appointment was especially difficult since he hadn't been for several days. David had retreated to the bedroom to lie down. He was hurting, in more ways than one, and Amy was at a loss as to how to help him. He was spending too much time lying down. He slept all day, was on the computer all night. He'd lost weight and was drinking too much. He spent almost no time with the boys or with her. For the first time since she'd married David, she truly didn't know who her husband was.

She was afraid.

Going into the study, she sat down at the desk and jiggled the computer mouse, bringing the screen up from sleep mode. She wanted to check the email and was thinking about researching some information about depression and PTSD.

When the screen came up, she found herself looking at a website that contained information about the status of military dogs. A link at the bottom connected readers to another website that actively worked to provide opportunities to adopt dogs that could no longer work in the combat zone. Dozens of canine faces peered out at her, some with their handlers, many alone in a kennel. Waiting to come home.

Amy sat back in the desk chair and contemplated the screen in front of her. David never talked about Soldier after that first night. But it was obvious that the dog was still on David's mind. That's why he had come to this website.

David was looking for information about Soldier.

Amy's fingers tapped lightly on the keyboard as she maneuvered through the website, then moved on to the link to the adoption service. She read and learned. She thought about her husband, the brave combat veteran who felt inadequate, weak and defeated at the knowledge that he had left a fallen comrade- and a friend- behind in Afghanistan.

She glanced again at the screen before her. It was ridiculously expensive. There was a maze of red tape and a mountain of paperwork to conquer.

But it could be done.

The next day Amy called the boys in for a meeting. Then, with their enthusiastic permission, she began making phone calls.

Eight weeks later, on Christmas Day, there was only one box under the tree, displayed front and center. The boys grabbed it and excitedly presented it to their dad. Inside was a note, addressed to David. All it said was "Put on your uniform. And get in the car."

Amy watched with David and the boys at the airport as, one by one, returning military personnel were absorbed into their family's outstretched arms. It was a carbon copy experience to the one they'd had six months ago. But this time, David was on the other side of the rail, part of the welcoming committee.

With a smile on his face, and tears in his eyes, David turned to Amy and the boys. "Thank you for this," he whispered as the line dwindled and the last of the soldiers came down the jetway. "This was the best Christmas gift." He cleared his throat. "I know I haven't been myself lately, and I'm so sorry to be making life so difficult for you all. It's just been so...hard. I've felt... well, I don't know what I've felt. Maybe lost is the best word to describe it. Inadequate. Uncertain. Like I failed somehow." He hung his head and shook it sadly. "I don't know who I am anymore. Without the combat zone. Without the routine. Without my comrades." Bending down, he rubbed his thigh down to his calf. "Without my leg." He took Amy's hand and squeezed it. "I've been thinking about how much I've lost. I've forgotten how lucky I am. I promise to do better. I love you guys. I really do." He leaned down to the boys, who were hugging his legs. "And thanks for sticking by your old man," he said and ruffled their hair. "Now, before I get all sloppy in front of these men, let's get out of there and go home for that Christmas turkey!"

He turned to go but a young Marine that had come off the plane stopped him. He saluted and then shook David's hand. "Don't leave yet, sir. Not all personnel are off the plane." He smiled and winked at Amy and then turned back to the gate, his arm around his wife.

"Oh, of course. Thanks for letting me know." David turned back to the jetway entrance as well, and Amy heard him draw in a sharp breath.

All along the corridor, soldiers had turned back. A woman in a suit and briefcase entered the jetway, holding a short leather leash. The line of soldiers snapped to attention, saluting smartly as a huge

German Shepherd moved into the doorway. Moving slowly to allow for his limping gait, the woman led the dog down the corridor and Amy watched with tears in her eyes as the dog came to stand before her husband.

"Captain Pollard, it is my honor and privilege to present Army Specialist Soldier." She paused, then said in a soft voice, "Retired." She handed David the leash and stepped out of the way.

David looked at the leash in his hand. Then he, too, snapped to attention and saluted his Veteran comrade. The dog held his gaze. Until David got down on one knee, his injured leg stretched out behind him, and opened his arms. Then the massive dog whined once, and leapt into David's outstretched arms. Amy smiled as the boys jumped into the huddle, grabbing the huge dog around the ruff. The dog sniffed, licked each boy, then looked up at her. His liquid brown eyes held hers. Then he turned back into David's embrace, and Amy heard him heave out a heavy sigh.

After a minute or two, David worked to struggle to his feet. Soldier leaned in against him, trying to push him up with his nose. David patted him. "Always the helper," he said, and the woman in the suit laughed.

"Tell me about it," she said. "I couldn't go into the women's restroom without him going in first to make sure it was OK. I have never felt safer in my entire life."

She turned to Amy. "Mary Monahan," she said and stuck out her hand. "We've communicated several times via email." Amy nodded as she took it and they shook. Then Amy reached out and pulled Mary Monahan into a hug.

"Thank you for this," she whispered, her voice thick. "Thank you so much."

Mary Monahan pulled away, but held Amy's arms in her hands. She looked into Amy's eyes and smiled. "No, Mrs. Pollard, thank *you*. This is a wonderful thing you've done. Our organization works hard to bring military dogs back to the States. They don't often get to come home to their handler, though. This is a special day for all of us." She reached down and ran her hand down Soldier's neck and back. "You've got your work cut out for you, too, you know." She handed Amy a sheaf of papers. "Here are his discharge papers and his certification for transfer from Afghanistan to the U.S. You'll have to have these certified by a veterinarian within three days and mail them back to the address listed on the form. There is also a list of exercises and medications he will need to help him continue to recover from his injuries." She handed them to Amy and looked into David's concerned face. "He took a beating, that's for sure," she said to David. "You all did. But Soldier's prognosis is excellent. He'll always walk with a limp. It will be up to you to determine how pronounced the limp will be. The more you adhere to the exercise regimen, the better off he'll be." She looked pointedly at David's leg and his cane. "But you already know that, right Captain?"

David looked at Mary Monahan with the unflinching gaze borne of years staring into a commanding officer's eyes. He knew one when he saw one. "I will make sure that Soldier gets the best care. He'll be good as new in no time." He looked from Mary Monahan to Amy. His eyes were full of apology and a new firmness. "We both will."

Mary Monahan nodded briskly. "Well, then, my work here is done. Time to get home, call the kids, get something decent to eat, then it's back to the Middle East. Kuwait, this time. I think." She shook hands with David and Amy, then bent to get her briefcase. Soldier immediately stepped between her and the briefcase, his body stiff, his eyes serious. Mary Monahan sighed. "OK, Soldier, one more time." She rolled her eyes as Soldier went over every inch of her briefcase, then stepped aside and sat. Mary picked up the briefcase, leaned down and looked Soldier in the eye. "Thank you for your service, my friend. Your country will never forget. Now, go home and be a dog."

"Soldier, look out. Stop wagging your tail like that or you're going to knock to whole thing over." Amy laughed as she scolded the dog, then hung the last of the ornaments on the tree.

She sat back against the couch and Soldier came over, lay down beside her and rested his head in her lap. The head of a rubber chicken hung out of his mouth, the only thing left from a Christmas present last year. His favorite. The mangled toy would show up in the darndest places- the toilet, her shoe, David's desk chair, Jonathan's cereal bowl. Amy had given up trying to get him to keep it on his bed. She shook her head and rubbed between his silky ears. Just one of the things you had to love about Soldier.

A year had come and gone since Soldier had come home. The change in the dog was amazing. He was healthy and spry, with just the hint of a limp whenever he was particularly tired. And his deep brown eyes shone with love and a quirky sense of doggy humor that made him just "one of the boys" around her house.

But even more amazing were the changes that Soldier had made in her family. Bringing Soldier home gave the boys a new sense of responsibility that had helped them settle and mature. They fed him and bathed him, ran miles with him in the backyard, whooping and hollering. And they stood by good-naturedly every morning while Soldier inspected their backpacks before they climbed on the school bus.

Having Soldier with him had given David the impetus he needed to finally come back from the front lines. He had taken a good long look at Soldier, then a good long look at himself. Within days he was back on his physical therapy schedule. He made an appointment with the Army psychologist and learned how to acknowledge and deal with his Post Traumatic Stress Disorder. He left the past behind, and began to focus on the future.

But, both David and Soldier were restless. Every day was regimented in Afghanistan. Now they didn't know what to do with themselves. For months, the focus had been on healing their injuries. Now they needed to work.

So, at Amy's urging, to work they went. An idea became reality after some long talks with David's commanding officer and an intensive training program for both he and Soldier. Now, they spent their days with wounded soldiers, helping them fight the good fight to feel whole again.   Both David and Soldier were where they belonged. Back on the battlefield.   But on an entirely different front.

As for Amy, she had discovered a mission of her own. She worked with Mary Monahan to raise funds and awareness that helped bring other military dogs home to their new families. She worked especially hard to bring those dogs back to their original handlers. Every time she did, she was amazed at the difference it made to the dog, the soldier, and their families. It made a complete circle. And brought a special joy to her heart. She was helping other military families make their houses into homes.

And, just a couple of weekends ago, Amy had unpacked the last of the storage boxes. She looked at the Christmas tree, decked in ornaments she hadn't seen in years. It made the holiday special. It turned the house into a home. Because Soldier had taught her that home was a special place that deserved the best of you. All of you. You could spend your life waiting. Or you could live for now. It wasn't really home until you were completely settled in. Until you had unpacked every last box.

As long as Soldier inspected them first.

When I wrote <u>Soldier's Homecoming,</u> I often found myself thinking about the thousands of military working dogs performing their jobs with dedication to a cause they don't even understand. What they do know is the meaning of friendship, of comradeship, of giving your all to those you love. They put up with the heat, the stench, the confusion and the fear without uttering a complaint.

What happens, then, when suddenly they are abandoned by those they've worked to protect? They will obey the commands they are given- but how do they feel?

This is Soldier's story from his own perspective. A perspective on war, and love, and what it feels like to be home.

<u>Soldier's Homecoming: His Own Tale</u>

<u>www.militaryworkingdogadoptions.com</u>

I am a soldier. That's what my Friend calls me. I don't quite understand what brought me to this hot, dusty place and I don't understand the Ugly. We work hard, long hours, sniffing into tight, airless places, always thirsty, always hungry. I have seen my Friend and his pack sleep in ditches, in corners of dark buildings, even standing up when riding the moving things that take us from place to place. It is a land of gloom even in the heat of the day. I sense the pain and tension in both my Friend's pack and in the many dark-skinned people that surge around us or hide when we approach. There is a bad smell here. It smells like fear. We are always ready to run.

I'm good at what I do. I can smell the sharp tang of the thing that explodes in a bright light and sends the sharp shards that pierce the skin and cause the blood to flow. And the blood is the same, whether coming from the dark-skinned ones, or the ones like my Friend. Even me. Whether we walk on four legs or two, the bright light and the smoke cause the fear to expand and then the blood to flow.

My job is to find the thing so my Friend and his pack can stop it from erupting. At least it was. Until the day when I found it too late and couldn't get my Friend away before getting hit by the shiny shards. In the midst of the screaming and the smoke, his pack mates grabbed him and pulled him away. He wasn't moving. I tried to get up to follow him, but I couldn't walk. Fire in my foreleg. And the blood. One of the pack heard my yelp and came back through the smoke for me, picking me up and struggling under my weight to lay me down next to my Friend in the back of the moving platform.

I lay close to him while people with most of their faces covered worked on us to stop the blood and the pain from taking us away. I lay close to him while our strength flowed back into our bodies. My Friend would stroke my matted fur and say soft things unless someone tried to move me from him. Then his voice would turn hard and his body would turn towards mine.

We didn't go back to doing our job. The rest of the pack went on without us, back into the heat and the Ugly. Then one day my Friend came to me in the place with others like me, all in wire rooms with their heads down and their eyes blurred. My Friend's eyes leaked water and that concerned me.

The only other time I'd seen him with water in his eyes was the day he'd carried one the dark-skinned small ones out of a place where the shiny shards had caught her. The blood dripped from her as he ran along the street to the people with the masks on their faces. He stayed with her. As her breath got smaller, his got deeper and faster and the water leaked from his eyes. Even when her breaths stopped, he stayed.

My Friend took me from the wire room where I'd been sleeping and put his face next to mine. We stayed that way for a long time. I was afraid to move. It felt good to be close to him again. To smell him. But the bad smell was there, too. If I didn't move, maybe nothing would change.

But it did. My Friend stood up and walked me back to the wire room. "Stay, Soldier," he said. He pointed to the room and I went in and sat. "Stay," he said again, and his voice made a funny cracking noise at the command. He shut the door, stood up and stared down at me. Then he turned and walked away. I am a good soldier. I do what I'm told. So I stayed. But, just for a moment, I couldn't keep the whine from escaping from my throat.

I'm afraid I became like the others around me. We were fed. We had water. The wire rooms were cleaned. My foreleg became stiff and I always felt the pain in it from lying on the hard ground and not being able to move around much. Others came and went. A few stopped their breaths. My Friend never came. But he'd told me to stay. And so I stayed.

Until the lady came. She was not like the others. She was soft and pale and round. Her voice was gentle as she walked around the room, commanding those with her. She went to each of those like me in the room and leaned down to look them in the eyes and speak quietly to them. Heads raised up and ears perked. When she got to me, I struggled to stand, but my leg was stiff and I couldn't get up. The lady turned to talk to one of the ones with her and he said, "Soldier" and "Captain David Pollard." She looked at me again and in her quiet voice she said, "Well, Soldier, would you like to go home?" I had no idea what her words meant, but she helped me up, put a leash on my collar and walked me out of that wire room and out of that dark place while those with her helped the others. I looked back and saw something I hadn't seen in a long time. Deep, clear eyes filled with hope.

Another wire cage and another dark place, cold and filled with a constant rumbling noise. I didn't want to be there, but I did what I was told. I am a good soldier. The soft lady wasn't with me anymore, but many of my other pack members were. I slept.

I was lead out into a bright day, but with none of the heat of the place I used to work. But members of the pack were there. They were dressed the same, they moved the same. But they smelled different. The bad smell was gone. The Ugly was gone.

I was confused. But only for a moment. Because then I smelled him. I turned my head and there he was. A female and two small ones were behind him. The lady tugged my leash and we walked slowly down the hallway and through a long line of people standing on both sides of us. As we walked, they all stood up tall and straight, raised their paws up to their foreheads with stiff fingers. Some eyes filled with water, some stared straight ahead, some looked down at me with a soft look. I found myself standing taller myself and found that my leg didn't move quite as stiffly.

We came to stand before my Friend. He leaned down to ruffle my fur and looked into my eyes with his. They were leaking water again, but I didn't sense the bad or the Ugly in him. He moved aside when his small ones knelt down next to him and held out their hands to me. Their voices were sweet and high and their skin tasted fresh when I licked the offered hands.

My Friend took my leash, then handed it to his female, who also looked soft, and kind. He then moved to the end of the line where he, too, stood straight and raised his paw to his forehead. I knew that position. It's what they used to do when someone important came along. Now they were doing it to me.

My Friend came back and took my leash. He looked down at me and said, "Come on, Soldier. Let's go home." I didn't know what that meant, but I was going with my Friend and that was fine with me.

No more heat and noise now. No more wire cages and endless waiting. No more Ugly. Now there is fresh food and water and a soft place for me to rest. It's never too hot or too cold. Soft hands rub down my sides and soft voices say my name and call me "Good Boy." My friend takes me for long walks with no job to do. We go to see the others in the pack that have bled and they stroke my fur and often leak water onto my back. It seems to make them better. The small ones bring me toys and tell me stories. This is home. It is beautiful. Everyone should be in one. No matter who they are or where they live. Maybe that's what all the Ugly is about. I don't know. But I know this is better than the Ugly. And I am glad I'm here.

‡‡‡

There is a child in an ashram in India, holding a stuffed bunny rabbit that once belonged to my daughter. Really. I wasn't going to give that rabbit away. I wanted to keep it, and the memories, for myself.

But we did give it away... and I am so glad we did.

Re-Gifting

I'd told her to clean up her room. Famous last words. Now, we stood like two islands amid a veritable sea of toys, clothes and stuffed animals.

"Well, honey," I said as I huffed out a breath. "I'm not sure this is my definition of 'cleaning up your room'."

"Yeah, but look at my closet," my 10-year-old exclaimed. "It's completely cleaned out!"

I looked into the closet. Except for the dust bunnies, it was indeed empty. "I can certainly see that," I said. But then I looked at the floor. "But it's not really clean if you just moved all the stuff to a different location. Perhaps it's time to get rid of a few things."

Hillary poked at a sparkly pink fairy wand with her shoe. "But mom," she whined, "it's my stuff!"

I bent down and picked up the wand. "Oh, come on," I said and pointed the wand at her. "You haven't played with this in years." I waved it over the mess on the floor and said "Abracadabra." Then I looked at Hillary. "See," I said. "It doesn't even work anymore."

My daughter was not amused. "That is part of my princess costume," she informed me and grabbed it out of my hand. She flipped a tiny switch at the base and the star at the top lit up with pulsing purple light. "And it does so work!"

I sighed a mother-of-a-10-year-old sigh. I spread my arm out to encompass the room. "Well, we can't keep everything here. We haven't even brought in all your Christmas gifts. Where are we going to put those?" I held up my hand as Hillary drew in a breath to answer. "That was a rhetorical question," I said and picked up the wand again. I touched the tip of the flashing star to her pert little nose. "Bottom line, Miss Hillary, you have to get rid of some of this stuff. Today. Otherwise, we'll have to send your Christmas presents back to Santa."

Hillary rolled her eyes. I didn't know whether to attribute it to the reference to Santa, the idle threat of returning her gifts, or just the fact that she had me for a mother. I didn't care. I put on my stern face. "Time to get to work. There is just too much stuff in here. Find the stuff that you're not playing with anymore and we'll get it to the Goodwill." I handed her the wand. "Here," I said. "Maybe this will help." I didn't stick around to listen to the response.

Now, let me just say that my daughter doesn't have *that* much stuff. She really doesn't. But Hillary is our only child. She likes to get fun things. And she does *not* like to give them away. She still has the rattles she received as a baby, claiming that she uses them for her own baby dolls. The fact is, she tucks everything away in some corner of some drawer, or in the deep recesses of her closet under the auspices of *you never know.* She gets that from her father, but let's not go *there.* It's my job as Wicked Witch to go in every once in a while and try to put some method to the madness that is her room. But, with Christmas just a couple of days past, and all the gifts still lying under the tree, the madness had to be reined in. Out with the old so we can be in with the new. I read somewhere that it's important to let the child have a say in what they give away. Yeah, right. But, I figured the task would keep Hillary busy for several hours, giving me time to get my own chores done. And get back to that new bestseller I'd gotten for Christmas.

I'd gotten to Chapter Four when I heard a scraping noise coming down the hall. I looked up to see Hillary bent over double, dragging a large, obviously heavy box toward me. The cat was chasing a pink feather boa that was trailing from the box.

"OK," Hillary said as she stopped to catch her breath. "What do you want me to do with this stuff?"

I got up and went over to the box. It was stuffed with an assortment of odds and ends. Barbie doll legs stuck up at impossible angles, their heads buried. Puzzles, book and boxes of markers and crayons were surrounded by stuffed animals, large and small. On top was a big, stuffed rabbit, soft and squishy.

I picked it up and held it out. "Oh, you're not giving this away, are you? You got this from great-aunt Louise when you were born." Aunt Louise had passed away since then. The rabbit held good memories of not only my aunt, but of Hillary as a baby, sitting on the floor, talking to the bunny in a language only they understood.

Hillary put her hands on her hips and narrowed her eyes. "You told me to get rid of some stuff. So, I did. Now you want me to keep it? You're going to have to make up your mind, mom. Because I'm tired and getting cranky and I really don't feel like putting all this stuff away again."

Despite the attitude, she had a point. I gave the bunny one last squeeze and put it back in the box. "OK, honey," I said. "Good job." I'll take it from here. You go on back and finish up. Then we can move your Christmas toys in."

Hillary turned and skipped back down the hall, anxious to get her new karaoke machine set up in her room. God help me. What was Santa thinking? Shaking my head, I lugged the box out to the car, shoving it in the back. I'd drop it off at the Goodwill tomorrow. Tonight, I knew I had several hours of listening to my daughter singing Taylor Swift's greatest hits over- and over- again.

The box rattled around in the back of the car for the next couple of weeks. I could see the bunny's head sticking up if I looked in the rear view mirror. I finally stopped at the Goodwill, going in first to look for a couple of sweaters for the cold yard work days. Passing through the toy aisle, I was amazed at all the stuffed animals, dolls and games. So much stuff. I felt vaguely depressed at the thought of all Hillary's toys getting lost among the toys already there. There were some great toys in that box. Good quality toys that would be great for someone who didn't have any to call their own. Not that I didn't appreciate the Goodwill, but I just felt like there was another way to get all those toys to a child in real need. Without the middle man. I found the sweaters I was looking for and drove away without dropping off the box.

I asked around at church and emailed some friends. Nothing. Every organization seemed to want new toys and clothes. No one wanted to take used toys, no matter what shape they were in. What a waste it seemed. I understood that some people used donations as a way to get rid of their garbage, but surely there must be a way to sort out the good from the bad. Most organizations weren't even willing to try.

Wondering how we ever lived without it, I turned to the Internet. It was amazing how many charitable organizations were out there, worthy causes seeking to help those in need.

What was even more mind-boggling was how much need there was. So much poverty, so much loneliness, so much pain and struggle. It made me sad to think of all the suffering in the world, but I took heart that there were so many trying to help. I wanted to be among them.

"Aha!" I said after an hour of searching. Finally. An organization serving the needs of families in India was seeking donations of usable toys for the children. A description of kids making balls out of plastic bags blowing by in the wind nearly broke my heart and, after printing off the pertinent information, I went off to get some strong boxes and packing tape.

Hillary's toys were going to India.

Packing up those treasures of Hillary's childhood was harder than I thought. I stood before two boxes filled with stuffed animals and light-weight toys. I held the big bunny out in front of me.

"Perhaps we should keep you around," I said, looking into his sweet face, the black button eyes gazing placidly back at me. "You'd make a perfect gift to one of Hillary's own kids someday." The dark eyes never wavered. "Oh, OK. You're right. Hillary doesn't care and it would be better for you to be played with than stuck on some shelf collecting dust because I was being a sentimental ninny." I gave the bunny a quick hug then shoved him into the box. The last thing I saw were those dark eyes. I hoped that out there somewhere was someone who would love him, as Hillary had. I sealed the box quickly, taped on the address and hauled both boxes out to the car. Before I changed my mind.

"$211.85? You can't be serious!" I stared in open-mouthed shock at the number on the screen. "They're just two boxes of toys! I don't think there's $211.85 worth of toys in there!"

The postal service employee looked out to the line getting longer and longer behind me. "Well, ma'am, that's the price. Would you rather not send them?"

I got the message. Either take it or leave it. But get out of the way. I looked again at the screen, the green numbers dancing in front of my eyes. My husband was going to kill me. I could think of a million things to do with two hundred dollars and change. But then I thought of those kids, just wanting to be kids for a little while. They had to grow up too fast. They deserved a toy to call their own.

"Fine," I said and swiped my credit card. The woman behind the counter stamped the boxes and stuck the customs labels on, then added them to the pile behind her. I had no idea if they'd even get where they were going, or what would happen once they got there. They might all end up in some corner of the customs office, undeliverable for whatever reason. Then it would be two hundred dollars wasted.

But the deed was done. I grabbed my purse and blew a quick kiss in the direction of the boxes. "Good luck, little bunny," I said. "Happy trails."

My husband was pretty philosophical about the whole thing. "Well, let's just hope they get to where they're going," he said with a shrug. "It's India. Who knows what their mail delivery systems are like. Maybe they're better than we think." He looked at me and sipped his coffee. "Bottom line- we'll never know what happened. Let's just hope for the best and let it go." He smiled at me. "Your heart's always in the right place. You did good."

When the credit card bill arrived, I thought about those boxes again, wondering if I'd done the right thing. I thought about the stuffed bunny, then thought about all the stuff in Hillary's room. I paid the bill, realized it hadn't even caused a blip on our financial radar screen, and promptly forgot the whole thing.

Next thing I knew, it was the holiday season again. I was browsing Amazon.com for some songs for Hillary's karaoke machine, thinking that I am nothing if not a glutton for punishment. The tree was up, the cards were out, and I was busy trying to get last minutes gifts purchased for everyone from the trash guy to my mother-in-law. Scrolling through the pages of songs for the karaoke machine, I had that vaguely nauseous feeling in the pit of my stomach I get every year when I think about all the stuff I'm buying, most of which I know will be in the Goodwill bin by this time next year. Sometimes I wished I could break the cycle, put an end to the useless purchasing and instead just invite everyone over for pizza.

As the karaoke song page blurred in front of my eyes, I thought back to the box of toys sent to India. I googled information on relief efforts in India and finally found the website I was looking for. Clicking around, I discovered an area with information and photos about the actual ashrams this group worked with. I was scrolling through photos of lines of world-weary, dark-skinned people waiting in long lines for food supplies when I stopped and stared.

"Hillary!" The word croaked out so I tried again. "Hillary!" I yelled and heard the thud of feet running down the hall.

"God, mom, what is it? Are you on fire?" Hillary skidded to a stop next to me. My husband was right on her heels.

"Good Lord," he said, putting his hand to his heart. "Are you alright? You scared the life out of me! Whatever is the matter?!"

I was still staring at the screen. "Look," I said. "Look at that."

Both Hillary and my husband bent forward, peering at the photo on the screen. My husband adjusted his glasses to see better.

Hillary sucked in a breath. "Is that..."

I released my breath in a long sigh. "Yeah," I said. "I think it is."

Hillary looked at me and I looked at her. My husband was still looking at the screen. He scratched his head. "Didn't your aunt..."

Hillary and I began to smile and we looked back at the screen. "Yeah," we said. "She did."

There, in the photo, stood a young girl, maybe four or five years old, thin legs and arms sticking out of worn, oversized clothing. She was standing barefoot in the midst of a pile of spread-out blankets, with assorted cans and boxes of food, clothing and other supplies laid out around her. Around the blankets sat a large circle of children and teens, all leaning forward eagerly. The little girl stood in wide-eyed wonder, her beaming white smile radiating in her lovely, dark-skinned face.

In her arms, she held a big, fluffy bunny rabbit. Hillary's rabbit.

The three of us stood there, staring at the photo, hardly able to believe it. Hillary wrapped her arm around me, and my husband reached over to squeeze my shoulder. We stared at the screen for a long time, flying across thousands of miles to a place where my daughter's old toy had found new life in the arms of another child.

All of a sudden Hillary said, "Oh look! There's my old sock monkey doll! And the My Little Ponies! And Elmo!" She pointed at different parts of the photo and, sure enough, there were more of her donated toys. We found plenty more, and it was obvious that both boxes had not only made the trip, but the contents were going to be given a whole new life.

The photo was tagged "Christmas in July." All I could think was that re-gifting had never felt so good.

Hillary and my husband finally left the room, shaking their heads in wonder and talking excitedly about how cool it was to see familiar items at home in a far-away land. I looked at the screen again, and smiled at the big, squishy bunny being squeezed in the skinny arms of a new friend.

I could swear he was smiling, too.

Under the tree Christmas morning was a big cardboard box with a big bow perched precariously on top. I looked at my husband, who shrugged. He hadn't put it there. Neither had I. Hillary was in the bathroom, singing "It's the Most Wonderful Time of the Year" in a high, excited, little-girl voice. I went over and looked for a tag. In Hillary's handwriting, written in red glitter pen, was a sticker reading "For the Kids in India." I lifted the flap on the box and saw the faces of a collection of Hillary's stuffed animals intermixed with a few toys. Stuck in the side was the fairy princess wand. On top of it all was a hand-drawn picture of Hillary, a big smile on her face. She was holding hands with a dark-skinned little girl holding a big, stuffed bunny. The little girl from the photo.

I thought about packing up another box. This one was probably bigger than the last. I thought about another two hundred-plus dollars in postage. I thought about my daughter sharing her things.

I thought about a little girl thousands of miles away, a child we would never meet, hugging a big stuffed bunny to her chest, eyes wide in wonder, a huge smile on her face.

I would certainly mail that package. I would haul that huge box to the post office, fill out all the forms and hand over my credit card without one single regret. Because that smile was worth every penny.

Hillary flew down the hall, yelling "Merry Christmas!" and squealing when she saw the tree. She ran to hug her dad, then wrapped her arms around me, squeezing me tight. We sat around the tree, handing out presents. The pile of wrapping paper grew as the wrapped boxes diminished. Soon, all that was left was the big box waiting to be mailed to India. We all looked at it and smiled. And I thought how amazing it was that the best gift under the tree was a box of used toys waiting to be given away.

I love to read, and one of my life's greatest joys was watching my young daughter, Emma, discover the magical world of reading for herself. I often volunteered in her classroom, and sat, spellbound, as student after student had that "light bulb moment" when the letters weren't just symbols on the page, but a <u>story</u>. It was glorious!

This story was my gift to the teacher and students of Emma's second grade classroom. Each student has a starring role in the tale, and, if you have kids of your own, you'll probably recognize many of the stories and characters. But to any kid, of any age, it's a reminder of the magic that can happen when you open a book!

So, call your child or grandchild, pull up a chair by the fire and let the magic begin!

<u>A LITTLE BIT OF MAGIC IN MR. K'S SECOND GRADE</u>

Magic (maj'ik) **n.** any mysterious power, producing extraordinary results.

For the kids of Mr. K's second grade class. And for the teacher who helps them know that the definition of magic is in the words.

It was a normal, sunny day about two weeks after school started. Hunter couldn't wait for quiet reading time. He hustled over to the bookshelves and grabbed his favorite "I Spy" book. Plopping down into the beanbag in the corner, he ran his hand over the book's colorful cover. He smiled. Today he would finally be able to find all the items hidden on page 12. Without help. Because today he could finally read all the words, all by himself. With that proud thought in his mind, he squished into the beanbag and opened the book.

That's when it happened. There was a small clatter as a handful of marbles, jacks and other tiny toys fell out of the book and into his lap. Stunned, Hunter, set the book aside and picked up the toys, let them fall through his fingers.

"What the heck," he said to himself. "This is really weird. It's just like..." Frowning, he picked the book back up and opened it to his favorite page. He started reading, following along with his finger. "Jack, toy top, four marbles, an army man..." Looking down in amazement, he touched each of the items lying on the floor in front of him. Hunter looked around, trying to see if any other of his classmates were having the same problem. They were all reading peacefully, some whispering to themselves as they sounded out the words.

"Uh, Mr. K?"

Their teacher, Mr. Knephoff, looked up from the pile of work on his desk. "Yes, Hunter, what is it? I'm kind of busy here."

"Well, it's just that, I mean, well, when I opened my book..." Hunter couldn't seem to find the right words.

"Is there a problem with your book, Hunter?"

"Well, no, uh, that is..."

"OK, then, why don't you go back and finish your reading. Quiet time is almost over. I've got some work to finish, too. And I know how exciting it must be for you to be able to read those pages all by yourself." Mr. K. lowered his head back to his paperwork and Hunter went back to his beanbag. He looked down at the pile of toys and at the pages of the book, not sure what to do next.

"Alright class, let's put your books away and come back to your seats." Mr. K. stood at the front of the room. He looked right at Hunter and raised his eyebrows. "I hope you all enjoyed your reading time."

Hunter laid the book flat on the floor, then piled the little toys back into the pages. Squeezing his eyes shut, he closed the book and held it shut for a moment. Then, peering from one eye, he opened it again, expecting all the toys to fall out. To his surprise, the toys were gone. Scanning the pages, he suddenly noticed the top, the army man and two of the marbles. He rubbed his eyes and looked again. Yep, there they were.

He shook his head and put the book back on the shelf. He'd hardly gotten to read at all. That thought made him stop dead in his tracks. How had Mr. K. known that he could read all the words in the "I Spy" book? He looked at his teacher, but Mr. K. was busy writing on the chalkboard. So, Hunter couldn't see his teacher's small smile.

Two days later, the class sat on the carpet and listened to Mr. K. reading from "Little Miss Spider." Kylee listened to the words, forming them like pictures in her mind. She had just finished reading another "Little Miss Spider" book and had been able to do it without having to ask her mom about any of the words. The story was great and now Kylee couldn't wait to read another one.

As she listened she turned to look out the window. Puffy clouds floated by in the blue, blue sky. Her eyes wandered until her attention was suddenly caught by a black speck dangling in front of the window. As she watched, the speck began to move, and she discovered it to be a spider, hanging by its silken thread. But not just any spider. Kylee sat up and stared. The spider had big eyes, and a smiling mouth- just like Miss Spider from the story! She looked over at Summer, who was watching Mr. K. and then over at Tanner, trying to get his attention. But Tanner was busy tracing the pattern on his camo pants and Kylee gave up. She watched the spider by herself for a while, then looked back to the book Mr. K. was holding up. In the picture, from this distance, it looked like there was an empty space where Miss Spider should have been.

Mr. K. suddenly shut the book with a snap and stood up. "It's about time for P.E., everyone," he said.

Kylee stood in line next to Summer. "Did you see that?" she said to her friend.

"See what?" Summer asked.

"Little Miss Spider. On the windowsill. Spinning her web while Mr. K. told the story."

Summer shook her head. "You're crazy," she muttered. She looked over toward the windows. "There's no spider, Kylee. You're seeing things."

Kylee looked at the window, too. Miss Spider was gone, but there was a piece of a sticky web stuck to the corner of the window frame. Kylee left the line and went over to Mr. K.'s desk. Summer followed.

"What are you doing?" Summer asked, peering over her shoulder as Kylee opened the book they'd just finished reading.

"There!" Kylee pointed to the page where they'd stopped. "There she is! It's Little Miss Spider, building her web. Just like she was on the window!"

"Of course, she's there," Summer sighed. "That's where she's *supposed* to be!"

"Ladies, would you care to join us in line?" Mr. K's voice was firm. Summer reached over and shut the book. Then she looked at Kylee, shook her head and grabbed her hand.

"You're seeing things," Summer said and hauled Kylee into line. "Let's go to P.E."

They moved with the line out into the hall, so they didn't see Mr. K. go over to the window, swipe at the web with his finger, and smile.

Over the next few weeks, the kids in Mr. K.'s class were super excited about Jog-a-thon and then preparations for the approaching holidays. So, they didn't notice the tiny fairy that flew by, the little monster that peeked from behind the computer desk or the flowers that grew by the drinking fountain. A few kids whispered about some odd things that they saw Mr. K. doing in the classroom- talking to the ceiling, shooing at something near the computer area or sweeping dirt and leaves by the sink. But no one paid much attention. They were busy with other things.

But there was no missing what greeted them first thing on Monday morning, the day after they returned from Thanksgiving vacation.

"Oh, wow!"

"What's that!"

"It's amazing!"

"I can't believe it!"

"It's huge!"

Kids were clustered around the door, staring inside, when Michael came up. He ran right into Nick, who looked at him with big eyes and his mouth open. His lips were moving like he was trying to say something, but no words came out. Nick moved aside so Michael could get near the door. He poked his head in, saw what was there, and shouted, "Oh my gosh! It's just like, it's just like... it's from a brontosaur! I just know it! The book I was reading yesterday said..."

His voice was drowned out as kids surged into Room 6 and formed a circle around the massive footprint oozing from the mud left right in the middle of the room. Desks were knocked over and shoved out of the way. The plants they'd been growing on the windowsills were gone, nothing left but short stems. And there was some kind of slimy stuff all over the windows.

"Oh, goodness, what have we here?" Mr. K. stood in the doorway, with his lunch in one hand and a bunch of papers in the others. The kids collected around him, talking full speed, asking questions and tugging on his sleeves to get his attention. All but Michael, who was staring at the huge, muddy footprint, holding a book about dinosaurs in his hand, flopped open to a page with a big, blank spot on it.

"I could finally read it on my own," he said numbly, still staring. "I was able to read about the Brontosaur and how they loved plants that grew in swamps and their footprints would…"

"Oh, so it was you that was reading the dinosaur book, was it?" Mr. K. came over and took the book from Michael's limp hand. The rest of the class huddled behind him.

Michael nodded slowly, his eyes huge. "And now the footprint is out of the book and… here in our classroom." Everyone was silent until Michael finished his thought. "That must mean that the Brontosaur…"

The class gasped and Mr. K. quickly took control. "Alright everyone, let's go and put your coats and backpacks away, while I call Ned. Come on, now, let's get busy!" His voice was suddenly stern and the kids moved out into the hall.

Mr. K. went over to the phone and placed a call. "Could you please send Ned for a cleanup?" he asked Sherrie, the secretary. "And have him bring the *big* bucket."

Ned, the custodian arrived within moments and maneuvered his way through the knot of kids in the doorway. He stopped when he saw the room and sighed. "Someone read the dinosaur book already?" he asked and Mr. K. nodded. "Well, better get this mess cleaned up," he said and moved his mop and big bucket into position.

"Alright, boys and girls, I think we'll head to the library a little early today," Mr. K. said quickly. "I'm sure Mrs. Zaugg won't mind. Everyone line up now. And don't worry, everything's fine."

"Easy for you to say," Gabriel heard Ned grumble as they were herded out into the hall. He pulled out a rag and swiped at the slimy mess on the windows. "Dinosaur boogers are darned hard to clean up!"

Madison walked slowly down the hall from the office, lost in thought. This was impossible, she thought. A dinosaur footprint in her classroom. Impossible to miss. Yet the teachers and other adults in the school acted as if nothing had happened. Like it was nothing out of the ordinary. They bustled and smiled and kept saying things like, "Alright everyone, let's get back to work, now. Lots to do." Madison shook her head. The kids in her class tried to talk about it, but Mr. K. was keeping them so busy with adding big numbers that they didn't have time to discuss this latest event. Or question all the weird things that had been happening almost since the beginning of the year.

Madison was thinking so hard about all she'd seen that day that she almost ran straight into the two 4th grade girls leaving the library. She hurried past them, barely seeing them. But their conversation suddenly brought her up short.

"I heard that there was a *dinosaur* footprint this time," one of the girls said.

"Yeah, with mud all over the floor and slimy stuff all over the windows," said the other, shaking her head. "We never had *that* in *our* class!"

They headed up the stairs and Madison stared after them. She heard one of the girls laugh and the other one said, "Yup, wish we'd had *that* in 2nd grade." Then she thought she heard them say, "We just had that one robot stuck in the closet. Good old 'Transformers'." But she couldn't be sure. She stood for a moment, waiting to hear more. But when the girls started talking about the books they had just gotten at the library and how they couldn't wait to get home that night to start reading, Madison shrugged and walked the rest of the way back to class.

Just before the holiday break, Lucas was walking back to class to get his coat before heading out to lunch recess. He stopped in the doorway as he heard Mr. K. talking to Mr. Sanders, the principal.

"I think we'll do the holiday read-a-thon on the last day of school," Mr. K. was looking over a calendar. "They've all reached the right reading level, so they've all experienced it, whether they realize it or not." Mr. Sanders nodded. "I was a little concerned about a couple of the kids; they were struggling a bit. But they've worked hard and it shows."

Mr. Sanders glanced around. His gaze settled on Molly, his dog, who came to school with him every day. Lucas looked over at Molly, too. The dog was busy sniffing at something in the corner of the room. Her tail was wagging merrily. As Lucas looked closer, he swore he could see a wriggling puppy hiding behind the bookcase. On Keegan's desk lay an open book. *The Pokey Little Puppy.* One of Mr. K.'s favorites.

Lucas turned back as he heard Mr. Sanders laugh. "Yes, it shows alright," he said. He thumbed through the stack of reading reports on Mr. K's desk. "They're early this year," he said. "Good for them." He set the reports on the desk. "Well, have fun," he said to Mr. K. He chuckled. "Just make sure everyone gets back to where they belong. It took us two days to find where Mary Kate and Ashley had gone last year. Quite a mystery." Lucas grabbed his coat and headed out into the hall as he heard his principal say, "Come on Molly, leave the little dog alone. You can play with her later. I'm sure she'll be around for a while."

Lucas stood hidden in the hallway, breathing hard, amazed and puzzled by what he'd just seen and heard. Mr. Sanders had seen the odd event occurring in Mr. K's class, and yet... he did nothing. What was going on here?

Outside, kids were huddled in little groups under the covered play area. Lucas spotted Bruce and Kyle over in one corner and headed toward them. Rain turned the school yard misty green and grey. The play structures and swing sets looked forlorn as rain dripped from their metal rungs and houses in the distance looked like old chalk drawings, fuzzy and washed out. Lucas reached Bruce and Kyle. "What are you guys looking at?" Bruce and Kyle were staring out in the distance. They didn't say anything at first, just looked at Lucas. Then Kyle pointed.

Lucas followed Kyle's finger out past the soggy baseball fields and out to the far reaches of the school property. He squinted to try and see through the rain and mist.

"Is that...?"

Bruce looked at Lucas and nodded. "Yup, I think it is," he said in a quiet voice.

"Well, what the..." Lucas couldn't believe his eyes. Way out near the far fences, a big oak tree rose out of the yard. At the very top of the tree, tucked into its sturdy branches, was a tree house. An odd, bluish light was coming out of the windows.

He looked at his friends. Kyle was just shaking his head. Bruce had a really weird look on his face.

"Well, who's the one reading the "Magic Tree House?" Lucas asked.

Just then someone bumped into him from behind. "Oh, sorry," a girl's voice said. The boys turned. Two kids scooted past them, one blonde, the other with glasses and a backpack. They were both wearing togas.

"Hi Bruce," the boy said as they rushed by. "Great to see you."

"Hi Jack," Bruce said weakly. "Hi Annie." Annie waved and smiled, then they were lost in the crowd. Kyle and Lucas turned to look at Bruce.

"So, it was you," Kyle said. Bruce just shrugged and gave his friends a little half smile. "Vacation Under the Volcano," he said. "It was the first one I was able to read without asking for help with any of the words. I finished it yesterday at reading time. And this morning..." He gestured at the tree house. The boys turned to look for Jack and Annie, but they'd disappeared into the crowd of kids. The bell rang and the boys had to head back to class.

It was finally time for the overnight read-a-thon, the class reward for passing all their reading requirements. Sleeping bags were scattered around the room. The air smelled like popcorn and leftover pizza. Paper snowflakes hung from the ceiling and handprint reindeer decorated the walls. Parent chaperones were out in the hall visiting, checking in from time to time. The windows of the classroom looked out onto a dark night filled with sparkling stars. Anticipation zinged through David and Ridge as they grabbed their flashlights and slid into their sleeping bags. Mr. K. had promised to finally explain all the weird stuff that had been happening, and they were certainly ready to hear it. Looking around, they could tell that the other kids were waiting too.

But Mr. K. was gone a long time and finally David and Ridge pulled out their book, a tale of a lost world and its amazing creatures. Ridge got out his flashlight and they began to read. It got quiet as the other kids began to do the same.

The two boys were reading the same book, taking turns turning the pages as they read to themselves. After a few pages, they heard a rustling behind them. They each took a deep breath and stared at each other.

"It can't be," David said in a whisper. "Can it?"

As one, the boys turned around and stared. Dark, dense trees stretched up above them. Moss drooped down and night creatures flitted through the branches, calling to each other. A low growl came through the dense brush and a smoky haze filtered through the leaves. The floor started to shudder under their sleeping bags as out of the trees came a huge dragon, with red scales and fierce eyes. He strode up to the boys, looked deeply into their faces for a moment, then lay down between their sleeping bags, his yellow eyes watching, his tail twitching.

The boys turned to see if the other kids were seeing what they were seeing, but it appeared that everyone else was busy. Kami and Hannah were dancing with 12 princesses. Tehya and Riley were lifting off in a rainbow-colored hot air balloon filled with toy bears. Lexi was peering into a moonlit meadow that was forming in front of her. Tiny lights flitted through the trees and one dropped into her hand, staying still long enough for Lexi to admire the delicate wings and gossamer gown of a tiny fairy. Jasmine was sitting near the window with a young, bearded man in long robes. He had a kind smile and gentle voice and was making beautiful gestures with his hands. Books were scattered around the room, left open on the floor, and the kids stared as the words and pictures on their pages shifted and melted, reforming fantastically in every corner of Room 6.

"It's magic," Sierra whispered.

"Oh, it's magic alright," Mr. K. said as he entered the room. The kids all turned to look at him. A little puppy followed him, his nose poking into every corner.

"Who did this?" Sierra asked. She walked toward Mr. K and her arms spread out to encompass all that was in their classroom. "Was it you?"

Mr. K smiled. "Oh, no, it's not me," he said with a shake of his head. He walked to his desk and sat down behind it. A fairy came and lighted on his shoulder. A long, green snake slithered close and lay at his feet.

Keegan stood up. "Well, if you didn't do all this, who did?" He scratched his head as a man in a space suit bounced by and waved. "Who can do all this?"

Mr. K. looked around the room, then his eyes settled back on Keegan. "You can," he said. "You, each of you, did all this."

The kids gasped in unison. The fairies giggled and the dragon snorted. Mr. K. stood up.

"Hunter," he asked, "when did you first notice that your book came alive?"

Hunter frowned. "You knew about that? But you acted like you didn't know anything."

"Oh, I knew," Mr. K. said as he helped himself to popcorn. "But you didn't answer my question. When did *you* know?"

Hunter thought. "Well, it was the day that I was able to read the whole list in the "I Spy" book by myself. That's when all the stuff fell out onto my lap. I could read the words by myself."

"That's it," said Mr. K. "That's when the magic begins." He looked at each of his students. "Reading is hard at first and you're concentrating on learning the words. You want to quit, you get frustrated, it often doesn't make sense. It's not really all that fun." He held out a finger and the fairy flew from his shoulder onto his finger. Then she flew over and settled on Lexi's arm. "But then, one day, in the middle of a sentence, something clicks." He shrugged when Audrey looked confused. She was new to the class and still a bit overwhelmed by all that she was seeing. "Maybe I'm not describing it right, but that's what happens."

"I know what you mean," Bruce said. "I remember when it happened. One minute the words wouldn't come together, but then the next minute-they did. And the story became- a story. Not just a bunch of words. It was great! And the next day…" He stopped and looked at Kyle and Lucas. "And the next day the book came alive!"

The kids all nodded. They looked at each other and looked down at their favorite books, then out into the room where their favorite characters were standing among them. A meteor streaked by Audrey's head and she stared in awe, then reached down and stroked the page of her beginner's astronomy book. "It IS magic," she said.

"It is magic indeed," Mr. K. said softly. "But it's magic that YOU make. Every time you open the pages of a new book."

Mr. K. stood up from his desk. Kids were turning on their flashlights and sliding into their sleeping bags. Ryan yawned as a huge, red Bionicle sat down at the end of his sleeping bag. Books were piled all over the floor, open to special pages, all blank except for the page number. Then, as the kids settled down, the characters and scenes melted slowly back into the pages from which they came.

"Does it only happen here?" Angelica asked as she stroked the sleek mane of the unicorn at her side. The unicorn nuzzled her hand and she giggled. "Is the magic only in this room?" She watched as the unicorn walked slowly to her fairytale book and slid down a rainbow and into the page. She sighed.

Mr. K. smiled and turned off the lights. A shooting star skidded across the ceiling of the classroom and burst in a flash of colors over Doris' head. A big, full moon laughed just outside the window. "Well, you'll just have to see, won't you?" he said. "Now, everyone, flashlights off. It's been a pretty busy evening. Let's all get some sleep."

Naomi closed her eyes, then opened them just a crack to watch her teacher slide into his own sleeping bag and turn off his flashlight. In the dim light Naomi saw the pokey little puppy snuggle up to Mr. K. In the quiet, she heard Mr K. say, "Shh, now. Lay down and be a good boy. Or no dessert for you." Naomi fell asleep with a smile on her face. And dreamed about the magic in her classroom. Just like everyone else.

A week into Christmas vacation, Emma's mom came down the hall toward Emma's room. "Honey, I..." She turned into the doorway and stopped. Four horses stood side by side, tails swaying gently. Emma was talking to three girls dressed in riding boots and helmets. One was holding the reins of all four horses. Lying open on the floor next to Emma's special reading space was the latest copy of the Saddle Club.

"Hi, Mom, look who's here!" Emma's voice rang with excitement. "It's Stevie, Lisa and Carole."

"Well, um, it's lovely to meet you girls," Emma's mom said. She looked a bit dazed as she stared at the horses filling up her daughter's room.

"Nice to meet you, too, Mrs. Ritter," said Carole with a big smile. "We were just asking Emma if she'd like to come riding with us." She handed a helmet to Emma.

"Yeah, there's always been only three members of our club," said Lisa, "but we've decided to make Emma our fourth member. She's great!"

"Did you hear that, Mom," Emma said as she put on the helmet. "I'm a member of the Saddle Club. Just like I've always wanted!" She turned to a beautiful dappled mare and stroked her mane, then looked at her mother. Her eyes were shining. "They said it can happen here, too," she said in a whisper. "Not just in Mr. K's class. Right here in my room. They said it can happen anywhere when I'm reading."

Emma's mom looked down at the open book, around at the room filled with horses and friends, then back at her daughter. She put a hand on her heart and took a deep breath. "Well, it looks like your reading is really coming along," she said. Then she walked into the room and went to help Emma up into the saddle. When Emma was seated, her mom looked up and smiled. "I'm so proud of you, sweetie."

"OK, girls, let's go!" Stevie, Carole and Lisa swung up onto their own saddles. Their horses snorted and swung their heads, ready to ride.

"Bye, mom!" Emma shouted as they rode out into the pink and gold evening light.

"Bye honey, bye girls," Emma's mom waved as the girls rode away. She leaned down and picked up the book, turned it over to look down at the blank page. She shook her head and rubbed a hand over the back of her neck. "Wow," she said softly. Then she looked at her watch. She set the book down on the desk and yelled out, "Don't forget to be done by dinner!"

Light, lovely laughter flowed from the pages of the book on the desk. From deep within the pages, Emma's voice yelled back, "I won't mom! I promise!"

THE END...OR THE BEGINNING!

‡‡‡

With grateful acknowledgement to the tellers of great children's stories:

- *Jean Marzollo, creator of the "I Spy" book collection*
- *David Kirk, creator of the "Little Miss Spider" collection*
- *Janette Sebring Lowrey, author of "The Pokey Little Puppy"*
- *Mary Kate and Ashley Olsen*
- *The Hasbro Company, creators of "Transformers"*
- *Mary Pope Osborne, creator of the "Magic Tree House" series*
- *Elana Lesser and Cliff Ruby, for the re-telling of "The 12 Dancing Princesses"*
- *Bonnie Bryant, creator of "The Saddle Club" series*

People say there aren't enough heroes in the world... I've been known to say it myself. But often we, especially our children, fall into the trap of trying to emulate those of questionable character, merely because they are the focus of current the media frenzy.

They fall flat, like a cardboard cutout. Because they have no real substance. They are living a lie.

How about if we choose to be the heroes of our own lives? What a marvelous aspiration! But before we can don the cape, we have to make a resolution to ditch our flimsy alter-ego and discover our real "superpower."

Then we can fly high. And others will have someone to look up to...

The New Year's Resolution

I am not a stupid woman. But sometimes I sure can act like one. How is it that you can think you know someone so well, and yet find out that you don't know them at all? Or, perhaps worse, you actually suspect that there's something not quite right, but you choose not to see it.

Life is a give and take. In order to get what I wanted, I never asked too many questions. I just took what came my way and adapted to a comfort level I'd never known in my entire life. I am the quintessential society matron. Polished, pampered. I say the right thing, do the right thing, show up in the right places looking smooth and glamorous. Quite the sleek façade. I have spent my entire adult life pretending to be someone I'm not. Smoke and mirrors. That's my life.

I've worked hard to get to this place. Now I'm dying to get out. Literally.

The foundation began to crumble on Christmas Eve. I was standing in the living room, nursing a vodka, watching the postcard scene of New York City framed by my penthouse window. A cold rain slid down the window, turning all the lights into a kaleidoscope of Christmas color. Perry Como crooned about those city sidewalks from the sound system hidden in the walls. Behind me, our own tree glistened and glimmered in a swirl of gold and white. No homespun Christmas here. Every decoration, every candle, every nut in every bowl was chosen and placed to portray the height of this year's definition of class. We were on display, just like the windows at Saks. My husband demanded a home that reflected both his position in society and his burgeoning income. Fine by me. I love the decorating. It just adds another fine layer to the pretense that is my life.

I glanced at my watch and took another sip. He was late. We were expected at the Jordan's home an hour ago. Drinks were being served. If we were much later, they would start dinner without us. Arriving in the middle of the soup course was sure to irritate Carole Johnson to no end. And I would spend the next six months trying to get back in her good graces. Great. Remembering how to kowtow to some snob who thought they were better than me was something I'd never forgotten how to do. But to have to do it now really chapped me.

Just as I was building up a good head of steam, thinking juicy thoughts about what I was going to say when my louse of a husband got home, the doorbell rang. I set my drink down a little too hard and vodka splashed onto my dress. Great. Just great. Now I would have to change before leaving. Thank goodness my personal shopper had talked me into the other cocktail dress as well. But it would take extra time to change. Darn him anyhow, I thought as I stalked to the door. And he hadn't even brought his key! What an idiot!

"It's about damn time, Wade! What..." I whipped open the door, ready to let my husband have it. Two vodkas and a ruined dress would set anybody off. But my words faded as I looked at the two men at my door. Certainly not Wade. These guys had thick wool topcoats on, and raindrops stuck to their cropped heads. Their faces were blank masks. They looked down on me from a great height. These were certainly not any of Santa's elves. I little zing of apprehension skittered along my skin. Something was very wrong.

"Mrs. Walters?" The man on the right stepped forward slightly and spoke in a deep voice that came from way down in his chest. He reached into his coat pocket and I flinched. I couldn't help it. He was a little too close and a little too big. For just an instant, I had this crazy notion that he was about to pull out a gun.

"Yes. I'm Audrey Walters." My voice cracked, just a little, and I realized I was chilled. I brought my arms up and crossed them in front of me and began rubbing my hands up and down my bare skin to get the circulation moving again. My blood seemed to have settled in my stomach, where it was competing for attention with the vodka puddled there, a distinctly unpleasant churning sensation. "What can I do for you?"

Guy Number One pulled a leather wallet from his coat pocket and opened it, showing it to me. A big, gold shiny badge was stuck to it. "I'm Special Agent Calaveri and this is Special Agent Michaels. FBI." He nodded at his partner, who nodded briefly at me. "May we come in?"

I balked. "No! Absolutely not!" What did these guys think I was? Stupid? I glared at them and then frowned. "How did you get up here, anyway? You have to have a special key for the elevator." I stepped back and grabbed hold of the door. Suddenly I was stone cold sober. And afraid. The agents didn't move. "I will ask you again- how did you get up here? If you don't have an answer for me by the time I count to five, I will be calling the police!"

Special Agent Michaels put his hand out. "Ma'am, we *are* the police," he said in a voice meant to reassure. Instead it increased my chill. "We obtained entry from the management of the building. After a call from your husband." He paused. "May we please come in? We need to speak with you about your husband."

I opened my mouth to speak, then closed it again. The mention of my husband snapped me into Propriety mode. I stood aside and motioned for them to come in. Leading the way into the living room, I indicated the couch. "Please, sit down. I apologize for the outburst, but you can never be too careful." My tone was back to calm and cultured. I straightened my back and smoothed my dress, hoping the vodka stain didn't show. "May I get you something to drink?"

The two agents looked at each other, and a silent communication passed between them. I felt that shiver again. Agent Calaveri said, "No, thank you, ma'am. We're fine. Thank you for inviting us in. Why don't you have a seat."

I sat on the edge of the plush club chair across from the agents, folded my hands in my lap and held my knees together. I may have looked the classy babe on the outside, but in my head I was cursing Wade blue in language I hadn't used since I left the Bronx. We were never going to make it to the Johnson's party now. I was going to be licking envelopes for every one of Carole Johnson's charity events for the next year!

Agent Calaveri cleared his throat and spoke in a calm, clear voice. "Mrs. Walters, it's important that you listen to us very carefully. And we will be happy to answer any questions that we can once we've explained the situation. "

I drew in a breath. Discomfort and confusion was giving way to irritation. I do not like being talked to like I'm a dim-witted child. Especially by someone half my age. "Agent Calaveri," I said in a voice that could have refrozen the ice cubes in my drink, "I am a 64-year-old woman of greater than average intelligence. Why don't you stop patting me on the head and just tell me what is going on. I don't have all day. I am already late for an important engagement. This apparently has something to do with my husband. Where *is* Wade?"

Agent Michaels sat back and crossed one leg over the other, visibly relaxing. Agent Calaveri let out a breath and looked at his partner. They both seemed relieved that they weren't going to have to get out the smelling salts and revive the "little woman." My words seemed to put them back on track.

In a dispassionate voice, Agent Calaveri said, "At 4:45pm this afternoon, your husband and several 'associates' were arrested on charges of embezzlement and fraud. Your husband was also charged with several counts of kidnapping and accessory to murder. Because this case is potentially linked to mob activity, the FBI is involved and your husband has been incarcerated at the Federal Building downtown."

There was absolute silence in the room. The clock on the mantle ticked off the seconds and far below, the hush of muted traffic sounds filtered up. The rain had turned to sleet, and each pellet pinged against the window like sharp little bits of glass. Embezzlement. Fraud. Kidnapping. Murder. The words pinged against my brain just like the sleet on the window. A huge and heavy weight pressed against me. I couldn't breathe.

The agent was speaking again. I focused on his mouth, as if reading his lips would help me absorb what he was saying. "...we have a warrant to search his offices and this home. An investigative team will be here in a few moments. We have authority to remove any and all information potentially pertinent to this case."

A few more beats of time, then Agent Michaels uncrossed his legs and sat forward in his chair. "Mrs. Walters, did you understand what Agent Calaveri has told you?"

I stared at him, then at his partner. A loud buzzing sound had begun in my head and I had to work hard to get words to form and move past my lips. I shook my head and croaked, "No Agent Michaels. I do not understand any of this at all."

Six hours later, I was finally alone. Christmas Eve has moved into Christmas Day. I was still in my stained cocktail dress, still freezing in the sleeveless, beaded top. I long ago finished my drink and had had several more. I had to go to the bathroom, but I couldn't seem to get my legs to move. Standing at the window overlooking the city, I could see the room behind me reflected in the glass. The apartment was a shambles. There was white powder on every surface. Computers, TV's, DVD's, even the phone was gone. There was not a piece of paper anywhere. Drawers were half shut. Muddy footprints covered the plush carpeting. The big hall mirror was smudged. Wires dangled. All the professionally wrapped Christmas gifts were torn to shreds. My beautiful Christmas tree listed to one side. Several of the delicate crystal ornaments lay shattered on the floor. Several have been taken for "evidence."

The chill overtook me and I began to shake all over. I could not wait one more second, so I pinched myself and managed to make it to the bathroom just in time. Sitting on the john, with a trash bucket clutched in my arms, I was peeing and puking at the same time. When I had finished, I just sat on the commode, drained, trying to figure out what the hell just happened. My husband was in jail. My house had been ransacked by professionals calling themselves federal agents. Even my Christmas gifts were trashed. Happy freaking holidays to me!

The tinny jingle of a cell phone roused me. I put myself back together and stumbled around, finally finding it in the pocket of the sweater I had been wearing yesterday, which lay in the bottom of the laundry basket. I'd forgotten to take it out when I'd changed for the party. That was the only reason I still had it; the crime scene investigators must have figured nothing incriminating would be hiding in the bottom of a pile of dirty clothes.

The ringing stopped, then a beep let me know a message was on my voicemail. I looked at the screen and saw a number I'm wasn't familiar with. I called it and, within seconds a man's voice came over the line.

"Mrs. Walters? Audrey?"

"Yes. Who is this?"

"My name is Gerald Herschier. I am your husband's lead attorney. Wade asked me to call and make sure you were alright. We wanted to wait until the FBI was done with your house so that our conversation wouldn't be overheard."

I held the phone away and stared at the screen. A tiny lick of flame had started at the base of my neck. I was thawing out.

Holding the phone back to my ear, I said, "You and Wade *knew* there would be police crawling over my home and you didn't even have the decency to call me? Where is Wade? Why hasn't he called me himself?" My voice was screeching and the flame was spreading into my belly, providing a heat that melted the chill I'd felt since the agents had appeared at my door.

Gerald Herschier cleared his throat and I could hear the lawyer tone slide in, slick and slow. "Mrs. Walters, due to the nature of the indictments against your husband, he is unable to contact anyone. He can only relay messages through our legal team."

"Mr. Herschier…"

"Please, call me Gerald," his voice was low and smooth, intimate. "I'm sure that, over the next several months, you and I are going to working together often. We should certainly be on a first-name basis, don't you think… Audrey?"

My name on his slimy lips almost had me running for the bathroom again as my stomach churned violently. I breathed in and out through my nose in an effort to keep from vomiting all over my phone. But that fire was spreading inside me, and Gerald Herschier's sleazy voice just added fuel to the flame. I was not numb any longer. I was steaming mad!

He took my silence for acquiescence, because he continued. "Wade has a list of things he needs you to do for him. It is imperative that you handle these items quickly and efficiently. Do not write them down and do not tell anyone what you are doing. Is that clear?"

The fire reached my brain and an inferno erupted in my head. Wade and his legal *team,* including this slimy ambulance chaser, had a *list* for me to do? I was to do them *quickly and efficiently*? So that Wade was not inconvenienced and his legal team could get to work on the pile of lies that would make up his defense? Oh, I didn't *think* so!

"Here's what's clear, *Mr.* Herschier." I spoke in a tone that dripped ice. "First, you can tell Wade that he can forget getting me to do one single bit of his dirty work. Second, he can rot in that jail cell as far as I'm concerned. And third- and I cannot emphasize this enough, *Mr.* Herschier- he can take you, his 'associates,' and his legal team with him straight to hell!" With that, I shut the phone and threw it against the wall. It shattered and fell in a pile under the tilting tree.

The crazy rage slipped away, leaving a cold, mean fury inside me. This husband of mine, this man I had married and slept with for 30 years, this man I had shared my life with, had turned out to be a liar, a cheat, a thief and possibly a murderer. Even without details, the accusations slithered across the floor of our home like deadly snakes, and I knew without doubt that they were true. Because, throughout our marriage, in the midst of all those intimacies, I knew in the back of my mind that Wade lived a shadow life. Things he did and said through the years suggested a "sketchy" character. But they flitted past my radar and I let them go without testing their authenticity. No rocking the boat, remember?

That acknowledgement made me angry all over again. But not at Wade. I was angry at myself. I had allowed myself to live with a man who defined the word *despicable.* I did it because I was happy with my own little life and, as long as my cocoon was decorated and safe, I was not going to go places where my mind did not want to go. Did that make me any less despicable than my husband? Was I not guilty of "aiding and abetting?" Did pretending nothing was wrong make it so? No, it certainly did not.

You see, I lived a shadow life too. Under the glitz and glamour, under the manicured nails and the highlighted hair, lived a girl from the projects in the Bronx who would have done *anything* to escape the life sentence that was prepared for me. If left in the squalor that was my "home," in the despair that was my family life, I would serve my time for a crime I didn't commit, except for the mere circumstance of my place on the family tree. People from the projects rarely got out.

But I did. Wade had crooked his finger at me from across the bar where I was working as a cocktail waitress. I walked on over, took his arm, and walked out with him. And had never looked back.

Over the years, I turned a blind eye as I held out my perfectly polished hand for Wade's money. I didn't ask, he didn't tell. Nobody got hurt, right? Well, it appeared that people did get hurt. Maybe more than that. I was no better than Wade.

That hurt. It disgusted me. But, as I looked about at the wreck that was my so-called "perfect" life, I realized something. Wade was in jail. He couldn't do anything to fix his problems, even if he wanted to. But I could.

Slowly, I went over and collected the remains of the smashed phone and dumped it in the trash. Then, I righted the tree and fixed the ornaments that were askew. When the lights glowed softly against the green and gold again, I went in, took a shower and changed into an old, worn sweater and soft jeans. I grabbed my purse and fled the apartment, knowing exactly where I could go.
Sometimes you needed to go back to where you were from to figure out where you needed to go next.

•••

You can take the girl out of the Bronx, but you can't take the Bronx out of the girl. Stacy Harrigan shook her head at the sight of the older woman coming in the door, shaking snow off her jacket. The weather was deteriorating rapidly. Most people were inside with their families and friends, relaxing over coffee and pie after the orgy of gift giving and eating that was Christmas Day. Not her, though. Stacy never missed an opportunity to pick up an extra shift. Extra work meant extra money. She needed every cent she could get. Plus, there was no one waiting at home for her, no gifts, no tree. Working kept her from thinking too much. Or feeling too much.

The diner was nearly empty, and Stacy watched the woman take a booth in the back, away from the windows. She always did that, whenever she came in. It wasn't often, but she'd been coming for years and years. Probably in her early 60's, the woman worked hard to look younger, with streaked blond hair, a perpetual tan and a toned physique. All professionally done and all designed to look real, even if it wasn't. That said a lot about the woman. Her outside appearance was designed to show the world a glossy, upscale woman of means. Yet, underneath the designer hair and nails, Stacy could see the tough girl that lurked underneath. This woman may live uptown now, but it was obvious to her that she'd grown up downtown. A girl from the projects, just like Stacy. But somehow, this woman had escaped. Stacy wondered how that felt, the escape. It was what she'd longed for her whole life, it was what she worked toward every day. Yet, at 32, she was still living in the same dump, still schlepping coffee and burgers at the same diner, still walking the ugly, vicious streets with her head down and pace fast.

Every cent she earned seemed to get eaten up with the struggle of living alone. Her meager savings account was not growing very fast, no matter how she scrimped and saved.

She sighed as she watched the woman slip her rings from her fingers and into her purse. Big diamonds, lots of gold. That's what this woman was used to wearing. But she knew for sure that she didn't want to be flashing them around this joint. She clipped her purse shut and wedged it securely next to her on the seat as Stacy came up to her with the coffee pot.

"Merry Christmas. Would you like some coffee? Sure is cold out there."

The woman looked up. She looked exhausted. Her eyes were bloodshot, but she tried to work up a smile. "Merry Christmas," she said as she turned her coffee cup over. "I'd love some coffee. Thanks. Black is fine." She rubbed her hands together. "You're right. It is really cold outside. Quite a Christmas Day. Everyone should be in cozied up inside with an eggnog and a fire." Her smile faded a bit. "So, what are we doing here?"

"Gotta earn a living," Stacy said a bit harshly. She took a breath and tried again. "Someone's got to keep the hash warm for the lowly and lonely, right?" She smiled and poured coffee into the woman's mug. "Would you like something to eat?" She assumed a snooty French accent. "The chef has prepared a Christmas feast, featuring something resembling turkey, mashed potatoes, gravy and cranberry sauce.

Comes with overcooked corn or peas and carrots. Free pumpkin pie for dessert."

The woman took a sip of her coffee and grinned. "How can I resist? The special sounds absolutely yummy."

Stacy grinned back. "Well, since the only thing he's made, I guess that makes it special."

The woman didn't miss a beat. "Then I guess I'll have the special."

Stacy didn't even bother with her pad. "Good choice," she said and headed for the kitchen.

The woman stayed for a long time, pushing her food around the plate, not eating much. She drank plenty of water, though, and ate her pie. Stacy watched her from behind the counter. The woman was pensive, but antsy. Something was sure rattling around in her brain. Stacy wondered about her, what her story was, why she wasn't with family or friends for the holiday. And why she had come to this little hole in the wall diner for her Christmas dinner.

The woman looked up and caught Stacy looking, so Stacy hustled over with the coffee pot. "More?" she asked to cover her staring. She picked up the woman's plate as the woman shook her head and covered her cup with her hand.

"No more, or I'll be up all night," she woman said. She sighed and added, "I guess I'd better take my check and let you get out of here. You must be closing up soon. Time to get home to your own holiday." She looked at Stacy with a question in her eyes.

"Oh, don't worry about it," she said as she put the check on the table. "It's just me and the TV at home. When the cable works," she added with a wry grin.

"Yeah, not much celebrating for me, either. But at least my cable works." The woman pulled bills from her wallet and let them with the check.

"Let me get your change," Stacy said and scooped up the tab.

"No, don't bother. Keep the change. Merry Christmas." The woman started to collect her things. Stacy was flabbergasted at the size of the tip.

"Oh, thank you so much," she said on a breath. "That is so kind."

The woman looked perplexed for a moment. "Well," she said, "you took good care of me on what has turned out to be the lousiest Christmas in history. That's worth a lot."

Stacy pointed a finger at the woman. "I knew it!" she exclaimed as the woman flinched. "I knew you were from the Bronx! You may not look it, but no one says 'lousy' unless they're from this side of town!"

The woman deflated, then shrugged. "Guilty as charged. I guess it just slips out now and again. No matter how hard I try to cover it up. It's in the blood. You can shine it up but you can't ever get rid of it."

Stacy turned serious. "Getting out... is it hard to do?"

The woman looked deeply into her eyes, then away towards the door. "It depend on what you're willing to do. For me, a rich guy came along and made all the right promises."

Stacy sighed. "Boy, I sure wish that guy would show up here!'

The woman looked at her strangely. "No, honey. You really don't." The moment stretched out. Then the woman smiled and reached to pick up her purse. "Well, I'd better get going. Otherwise, I'll be another snowman out on the street!" Suddenly, her face fell and tears seemed to fill her eyes. She looked so vulnerable, so small and so filled with pain. She cleared her throat and stuck out her hand. "Merry Christmas," she said. "I hope your cable is on when you get home. "

Stacy tried to smile but it fell flat. She took the woman's hand and held on. Something, some bond, passed through them. Two strangers who knew the other's pain, and understood it. Growing up hard, wanting to get out of the poverty and violence and *hopelessness* so badly you could taste it. You could see the other side of the tracks, but getting across them was a long, arduous, often futile journey. They looked at each other. Stacy suspected the woman had gotten across the tracks but had paid a hefty price. She herself was still stuck, but with her scruples intact. She was pretty sure neither was certain who'd gotten the better deal.

Still holding her hand, Stacy said, "My name is Stacy."

The woman paused. "People around here always called me Audy," she said.

"Well, it's nice to put a name with the face," Stacy said. The woman seemed startled, and Stacy laughed. "I've seen you in here before. You're not like the usual clientele here."

"Oh," the woman said. "I guess I've always been a sucker for a rubbery piece of turkey-like substance covered in paste that was meant to be gravy." She smiled and Stacy laughed.

"Well, Merry Christmas," Stacy said. "And I hope you have all the best in the New Year."

The woman stared hard at her. Something seemed to click inside her. "Yes. The New Year. It's just around the corner. New beginnings." She pulled her coat around her and pulled on her gloves. "Happy New Year to you, too. I hope it's the beginning of good things. For both of us."

Stacy watched her walk out the door and disappear into the swirling snow. The dark street swallowed her up. Stacy stood for a moment, wondering what could make a woman like that so sad. Funny, she thought, how someone could seem to have it all on the outside, but was hollow on the inside. Missing the vital parts. She looked down again at the pile of bills in her hand. A windfall. Maybe this new year would be the beginning of better things after all. She pocketed the tip and hustled to get the table cleaned.

•••

Time at the diner made me feel somehow "right" again. I trundled along on the subway, then took a cab back to the apartment. I could see the news cameras and video trucks from two blocks away.

"Looks like a circus," the cabbie said. "I wonder what happened. Maybe somebody died?" He turned to look at me, while I stared straight ahead into the mess that was now my new "normal." I knew those cameras and microphones were meant to aim at me. The cabbie's words rumbled around in my brain, bouncing around like marbles in a pinball machine. "Somebody died, somebody died..." I mentally shook myself and tried to think.

"Yeah, looks pretty crazy," I said as nonchalantly as I could. "This is my stop. Let me out here." I took bills from my purse and opened the cab door.

"Sure thing, lady," he said. He took the money, executed an illegal u-turn and crawled away from the snarl up ahead.

I managed to skirt around and enter my building through the service entrance. Our night doorman, Enrico, was having a coffee break in the lounge when he spotted me. He scurried over, and used his key to open the service elevator.

"In here, Ms. Audrey," he said in a low voice. "Everybody's waiting for you. Not a good scene." He held the door and shielded me from prying eyes with his big body. His kind eyes looked into mine. "You need anything, you call me. I'll try to help. And no one will know. You can count on me."

I looked back, and thought fast. Enrico was as honest as the day was long. A good-hearted man, he was also quite resourceful. I could trust him. Of that, I was sure.

"Enrico," I said in a low voice from the back of the elevator. "I *can* use your help. I need a phone. And a computer."

"One hour," he said, as the elevator doors slid shut.

With the computer and the phone I was able to see what was going on in the outside world, even as I huddled in my apartment. I couldn't leave without being swarmed by the press. Wade's arrest was all over the news. Reporters camped outside the building in the freezing cold and deepening snow. I'm sure the phone would have been ringing off the hook, but the FBI had taken it. Thank God. No one had the new phone number, so the phone never rang.

Since no immediate family member was available for comment, the scavengers in the press went after whoever was willing to talk. Wild stories ensued, people gossiping madly in front of a camera, making up whatever would get them their five minutes of fame. Enrico, true to his word, kept the reporters away from me and pretended not to speak English whenever he was asked a question. He would look straight into the camera and say, "no comprendo" as if he were speaking directly to me, letting me know that at least one person was looking out for me.

I wandered around the apartment in a daze. The conversation in the diner popped into my mind at odd times. While I was trying to make sense of what was happening around me, I found myself thinking a lot about what had brought me to this place. It seemed that I had traded one miserable existence for another. In compromising myself to have the money and comfort I thought I craved, I had given up my self-respect, as well as my backbone. I thought about Stacy the waitress, her tired eyes, her sagging shoulders. The loneliness that poured off her, even though she was open and sociable to me. I knew where the loneliness came from. When trying to escape the Bronx, it was vital to keep your distance. Opening your heart to someone just tethered you to the tragedy that was life in the projects.

Both Stacy and I were still stuck. And I wasn't sure which one of us was worse off.

Outside my window day turned to night and back to day. I sat wrapped in the middle of the big, soft couch that looked out over the city. But I couldn't see anything. I couldn't feel anything. I didn't have any clear thoughts. I just sat. And sat. Depression sounds so heavy- it's a word I never would have associated with myself. But there was no other way to describe the sense of disconnection I felt. The world went on around me, but I had stepped aside to let it continue without me. Who cared anyway?

I had a new definition- the stupid wife of a thief and murderer. The blond bimbo who didn't open her eyes enough to see what her husband was doing. The aging escapee from the Bronx who looked the other way while her gravy train mowed down everything in its path, destroying lives, hurting others. I was overcome.

When I got up to go to the bathroom, I walked past the computer and looked at the latest news stories. Wade's escapades continued to make headlines. Names of his "associates" were made public, but I didn't recognize any of them. Innuendo suggested that they were tied to the Mafia. My husband's official business photo was often placed next to a video clip of him in handcuffs headed off to court. Oh, how the mighty had fallen. And with every "no comment" shouted out to the media as he was hustled away, I felt more and more disconnected. "No comment" was the fact of our marriage, the bottom line of our thirty years together.

I was completely in the dark about what was happening, and completely alone. Agents Calaveri and Michaels had been up once, after Enrico had gotten my permission, looking for any additional information that I did not possess. When I asked them about the case, they hemmed and hawed until I showed them the door. Agent Michaels tried to question the state of my emotional health, but I just closed the door in his face. What did they think my mental state would be?

Another night crawled into day. Sunlight streaming through the window hit one of the crystal ornaments and flashed into my eyes. I looked over and saw a rainbow shoot through the fine glass, arcing in a zap of color. I pushed myself into a sitting position and shoved the cashmere throw off of me and onto the floor. Every muscle in my body ached and my head splintered into a thousand pieces. My tongue was stuck to the roof of my mouth and I smelled terrible.

My eyes focused as I stretched, trying to relieve the sore muscles, and I noticed that my beautiful tree was dried out and listing miserably to one side again. The huge pile of gifts was still under the tree, but they'd all been ripped open when the agents had come searching for evidence of Wade's crimes. Instead of a beautiful, gracious holiday scene, it looked like something that fell out of a trash can. All the work, all the effort I'd put in to make the holiday beautiful- and it all looked like a windy street corner in the Bronx. A pile of discarded trash. Just like me.

That thought sounded ridiculously pitiful, even to me. This is what I'd been reduced to- a depressed old bag hiding from the pointing fingers of the great citizens of New York City. All at the "most wonderful time of the year." Anger shot through me like a bullet, hot and sharp. Damn Wade! How dare he do this to me! How dare he ruin my Christmas, make a mockery of my work and effort! Well, screw him! I went over to the pile of gifts and thought about tearing in.

But suddenly, I felt lightheaded. The room whirled around me, and I staggered over to the hall table and hung on. When my equilibrium returned, I opened my eyes. Right in front of me stood the most haggard face I have ever seen in my life. I gasped as I stared at myself framed delicately in the gold filigree mirror that hung above the table. Behind my stringy hair and sallow skin, the living room was a shambles. I knew the rest of the apartment was no better. I felt the backbone I'd abandoned beginning to grow back and I straightened my spine. Enough was enough! Wade may have screwed up my life, but there was no way in hell that I was going to help him along by wallowing in self-pity and fear. Not for one more minute!

Nutrition, in the form of scrambled eggs and toast, stopped the room from wavering. A thirty minute shower and several long glasses of water rehydrated my depleted body. Fortified and sane again, I muscled my way through the detritus of my apartment until every surface gleamed. After righting the tree and giving it a drink, I turned the lights back on and braved opening the front door to haul the garbage to the trash chute.

Taking another mug of life-affirming coffee, I went back into the living room. Life made sense again. My world was ordered and clean. Even the tree seemed to be coming back to life. The scent of coffee and pine was energizing and refreshing. It looked like Christmas. It smelled like Christmas. I felt like myself again. Or at least a version of myself I could live with.

"Well, Santa," I said to the large, tasteful white china statue standing next to the marble fireplace mantle, "since I've been such a good girl, I think I deserve to open a few presents. Don't you agree? Yes, I thought you might!"

Rubbing my hands together, I knelt beneath the tree and grabbed a box, shook it like a little kid, then tore in. Flinging open the contents, I threw the lovely cashmere robe on the sofa and grabbed the next box.

For the next hour, I pawed through every box under the tree. I didn't even bother looking at the tags. As far as I was concerned, they were all for me.

The last box didn't have a tag on it. I shook it, and heard a faint rattle. Ripping open the paper, I discovered a box for an iPad. I reached over for a letter opener, but when I went to slit the sealing tape, I discovered that it had already been opened, then made to look like it was still sealed. Darn it, Wade had bought used goods. Idiot. I opened the box and drew out the iPad, setting aside the operating instructions. As I did, a small key, like one for a locker at a gym, tumbled out. Thin, with an orange plastic plug at the top. A number 30 was inscribed in it I held it for a moment, feeling a tug of memory. I felt like I'd seen a key like this before. But the memory wouldn't form, so I set it aside. I turned on the iPad to see if it would work. Surprisingly, it came on right away and indicated a full charge. When the main screen settled in, I noticed there were all the usual programs and apps loaded in.

Plus one recently created folder. Hmmm.

Intrigued now, I tapped on the folder. It opened to a page filled with numbers, line after line of them. Scrolling down, I couldn't find any identifying information or any clues as to what the numbers were. I looked to see when the folder was created and found that it had been entered on December 15th. I tried to see who owned the iPad, thinking that perhaps it had been resold to Wade and someone had forgotten to clear the memory.

But the iPad was registered to Wade Walters, my Wade Walters. It had been registered and activated on December 15th. Nine days before he'd been arrested.

I sat back and finished my coffee, staring at the little screen and all those numbers. Then, leaning down, I rooted through the box and found the key. Holding it in my hand, I rolled it back and forth in my palm, thinking, thinking. I still could swear I'd seen a key like this somewhere before, but for the life of me I couldn't place it.

As for the information on the iPad, I knew in my heart that this information related somehow to all the trouble Wade was mixed up in. Some sort of weird, spy-vs.-spy code. Information about theft, embezzlement, perhaps murder. All sitting under my Christmas tree, hidden in plain sight. My lying, cheating, thieving husband had brought his dirty dealings into our home and left it to soil our Christmas! My blood pressure skyrocketed until I literally began to see red. Using language unbecoming my station in society, I dumped the box on the couch and stalked back into the kitchen to get another mug of coffee.

That's when I realized the date. It wasn't Christmas anymore. It was New Year's Eve. A week had gone by since my home, my life, my future, had been trashed, while I sat on the floor like a lump of coal dumped from a stocking. I had made it so that both Wade and I were in jail. A prison of my own making.

Shock and shame had rendered me incapacitated. My life would never be the same. But, how the changes came were entirely up to me. I could roll over and play dead, let Wade's disaster consume me. Or I could stand up, shake off the dust, and decide what I was going to do with my life.

It was New Year's Eve. So I made a resolution. A New Year's resolution. I would get to the bottom of this whole mess. I would find out what the note meant. I would find where that key fit.

And then I would make Wade and his "associates" pay.

Well, the anger and need for revenge fizzled after a while. Despite my roots, I'm just not the vengeful sort. But I was serious about the resolution. I would get to the bottom of this. And I was crazy curious about the information I'd found. I held the key in my hand, turning it over and over in my palm. Something was scrabbling away in the back of my mind. I'd held a key just like this before. Try as I might, I couldn't figure it out. Feeling frustrated got me feeling antsy. It was time to get out of the house. Calling down to the desk, I asked for an update from Enrico.

"Well, Ms. Audrey, there are still a few news people out front. Most have given up... too cold for them out here and we won't let them into the building, even to use the facilities, if you know what I mean." He chuckled. "There's no easier way to get rid of stoop warmers than to make them hold it."

I laughed with him, a strange sound in my ears. "Well, what do you think? Can I sneak out?"

Enrico was quiet for a moment. I could hear the wheels turning in his head. Then he said, "Come down to the third floor. Go to the laundry room. I've got a plan."

The plan turned out to be sneaking me out in a laundry cart to the back loading dock. He handed me the keys to his car, a plain blue sedan. "Just be back by midnight, or it turns into a pumpkin," he said with a wide grin. "So do I... it's the end of my shift and I will be more than ready to head home and rest these bones."

I hugged him. "Thanks, Enrico. You are the best. I don't know what I'd do without you!" I climbed into the car and opened the window. "I'll bring you back some pie, how's that?"

"Pecan," he said without missing a beat. "My favorite. Nothing better with a shot of good whiskey at the end of a long day." He smiled and made a shooing motion. "Now go!"

I blew him a kiss then rolled up the window. Turning the key in the ignition, I cranked up the heat and sped off into the late afternoon chill.

•••

Stacy blew in the door of the diner, followed by a cold gust of wind. She stamped her boots off on the carpet, and surveyed the patrons as she took off her gloves. Most people were out getting ready for New Year's Eve festivities, but a few old regulars held down their

107

usual spots at the counter, huddled over endless cups of coffee, ticking off the endless, lonely minutes of their lives in the company of strangers they pretended were friends. This part of the Bronx was like that. Many of these folks had learned the hard way that giving your heart often led to it breaking in a million pieces- family fled the projects or died in the streets, neighbors hid inside their homes, fearful of the violence that littered the hallways and alleys surrounding their apartments. So, when the day sat too oppressively on them, these folks shuffled down to the diner, where at least they knew what to expect. They existed in an unsettled kind of camaraderie. Stacy knew how they felt. It was her existence too.

She had just hung up her coat and picked up her order pad when Audy, her Christmas angel, appeared in the doorway. Flushed and a bit breathless, she looked quickly around the diner, shot a hurried glance over her shoulder back into the street, and then scurried to a booth in the back. The busboy brought her coffee and water, and dropped a menu on the table. Audy looked up briefly, nodded her thanks, then pulled some sort of tablet out of her purse and turned it on. Taking sips of the scalding coffee, she sat studying something on the screen of the handheld device.

Stacy shook her head, thinking that having something like that out here in a place like this was asking for trouble. People had fast hands in this neighborhood. It would be gone in a flash if Audy wasn't careful. The front door opened again and Stacy went to seat the dark-haired man in the leather jacket who had just come in.

•••

"Can I get you some coffee? It sure is cold out there today." Chris Mancuso looked up at the waitress, smiled briefly at her blond, pretty face, and nodded. Her nametag read "Stacy." He thought the name fit her. Youthful. With a touch of feisty.

The waitress poured the coffee, then nodded at his menu. "Do you know what you want, or do you need a few minutes? The special today is turkey and mashed potatoes." She looked at the kitchen, then lowered her voice. "I don't recommend it."

Chris looked at her more closely. "Cute. With a sense of humor." His blue eyes sparked as he watched the waitress blush. He picked up the menu, scanned it briefly and snapped it closed on the table. "Burger," he said. "With chili fries. And pie. Bring it all at once."

Stacy laughed. "Cute. With a sense of indigestion," she said and Chris's lips twitched. He couldn't help it. This one *was* feisty. He liked that. Just for kicks, he turned his full wattage smile and her and watched her face for a reaction. He certainly got one. She melted, just for a split second, then froze up. Just like closing up shop, he thought. Too bad.

"I'll get that right away, sir," Stacy said in a chilly voice and headed off to the kitchen. Chris took a moment to watch her go, feeling a nudge of regret. He wished... well, it didn't matter what he wished sometimes. He lifted his coffee cup and turned his focus on the woman in the back booth frowning over something written on an iPad.

•••

"You really are a holiday reveler, aren't you?" Stacy approached Audy in the back booth, surprised when she jumped. "Sorry, didn't mean to startle you. It's just that the last time I saw you was Christmas night. Surely, there must be more upscale places for you to spend your holidays. Although," she said with a wry grin as she looked around, "this place does have a certain 'Charlie Brown Christmas' kind of appeal. But it's not much for New Year's Eve."

Audy smiled, a thin, rather sad smile. "It's all in how you look at it," she said as she looked around. "One woman's dump is another woman's palace."

Stacy thought about that for a moment. Something about this woman seemed so out of place here, yet so at home. "Well," she said, "to each their own." She leaned over to fill Audy's coffee cup and her gaze settled on the iPad. She smiled. "Oh, you like anagrams, too? I just love the challenge of unraveling the code." She tapped the side of her head. "Gives the brain a challenge, you know? Kind of a mystery, like a secret language. I..." She dropped off as she saw Audy staring at her. "Um, sorry," she said, stumbling over her words. "I didn't mean to snoop. It's just that..."

"You know what this is?" Audy asked with an odd look on her face.

"Well, it looks pretty simple. Kind of a classic. At least for those who like this sort of puzzle." She looked at the puzzle, then back at Audy. "Don't you know what this is?"

Audy shook her head. "No, no I don't," she said. "I have no idea what it means. Is it some sort of code that translates into words?" She pushed the iPad in Stacy's direction. "Can you figure out what it says?"

Stacy frowned at the serious look on Audy's face, then peered again at the numbers on the page. "It looks pretty standard. A number correlates to a letter. The spaces are where words form. See?" She indicated spaces with her finger.

Audy put her hand over Stacy's wrist. Her fingers were freezing cold. Her eyes locked on Stacy's. "Listen, Stacy," she said in a low, serious voice. "I made a New Year's Resolution to figure out what this bunch of gibberish means. Do you think you could decipher it? There is a very handsome tip in it for you if you can." Her grip tightened. "And I would be *very* grateful. "

Stacy saw a rawness in the woman's eyes. Whatever was on this page was very important to her. She looked back on the iPad screen and nodded slowly. "I'm sure I can figure it out," she said. "It just requires figuring out what numbers represent which letters. That will take a few tries, but once certain words come together, it gets easier." She smiled at Audy, trying to set her at ease. "Just let me get my orders up and I'll show you." She looked down at

Audy's hand over her own wrist. "It'll be OK, I promise. It's really not that hard, when you know what you're doing." She gently removed her hand and patted Audy's. "Sit tight and I'll be right back."

Audy's eyes drifted back to the screen. She nodded, lost in a daze. Stacy patted her hand again and turned to head back to pick up her orders. Her gaze landed on the dark-haired, blue-eyed man in the front booth. He was staring intently at Audy. His eyes locked with Stacy's and Stacy's breath caught in her throat. She stared back, and he smiled insolently, then turned to stare out the window, dismissing her. Stacy hurried to the kitchen, picked up his burger and chili fries, grabbing his pie from the cooler.

But when she turned to bring his food to him, she found his table was empty. The man was gone. On the table was two twenty dollar bills. He'd paid his bill. He wasn't coming back.

•••

Chris turned the corner, then pulled his cell from his pocket. Punching a button, he stopped in a doorway, trying to get out of the wind while he waited.

"Yeah, it's Mancuso," he said without preamble when the phone call connected. "She's actually out and about." He listened. "No, no one's with her, she's alone." Another pause. "Just some diner in the Bronx, having coffee, playing with a new iPad. I don't know what's on it, but I'm guessing it's the stuff." He looked back toward the diner as he listened. "Yeah, yeah, I'll stick with her. Nah, she didn't even notice me." He thought about Stacy the waitress and how *she* had noticed him. But he shook it off. She wasn't important. His job was to take care of Audrey Walters. There was a lot riding on whatever was on that iPad.

He finished his conversation and snapped his phone shut. Then, pulling up the collar of his coat, he stuffed his hands deeper in his pocket, and lounged in the doorway, oblivious of the revelry going on around him. His gaze was focused solely on the door of the diner.

•••

Stacy took the burger and fries over to Audy, setting the plate down in front of her. Audy looked up with raised eyebrows. "On the house," Stacy said. "Happy New Year."

Audy looked down at the mass of food on her plate. "Good Lord," she said in awe, "I haven't eaten like this in years!"

"Well, then you'll really enjoy that pie that comes with it," Stacy said and set the plate down next to the burger. "Eat hearty, and I'll be back in a few."

Stacy watched Audy stare at the plate, shake her head, then dig in with gusto.

Around 10 pm, the diner emptied out and Stacy's boss left her to finish the last of the cleaning and lock up. With the last dish put away and the counter wiped down, Stacy brought the coffee pot over to Audy's booth and sat down. The front door was locked and the lights were turned down. An old

TV flashed out scenes from Times Square, the sound a low blur.

"OK," Stacy said as she filled their cups. "Let's see what we've got." She held her hand out and Audy gave her the iPad. "Wow, pretty cool. I've seen these, but never really used one."

Audy looked at the iPad, and frowned. "A Christmas gift," she said. "But I'm not sure who it was for." Stacy looked at her with confusion and Audy laughed. "Long story," she said. "This puzzle is part of the 'gift.'"

Stacy looked at the numbers, then took out a pencil and began to scribble on a blank page of her order pad. This was her forte. Whenever she had time, she did puzzles like this- sorting out clues, putting sequences of numbers and letters together, solving the riddle. She'd done it since she was a kid. It came easy to her. Now a hobby could possibly help somebody out- and get her a nice tip. That, along with the tip from the dark-haired runner, would start her new year off right. Maybe, just maybe, this would be the year she could finally escape.

Thoughts flew through her head as she worked- her loneliness, her driving desire to get out of the Bronx, her neighbors, the kids on the street. The vicious cycle of poverty. Nearly every road was a dead end. Some kept trying. Some gave up. She felt especially sorry for the kids. Such potential wasted. That was one of the reasons she'd never married, never had children. There was no way she was going to bring a child into the projects. But that resolve didn't keep her from wishing.

She shook her head, then looked down at her pad. Sitting back, she pushed the pad toward Audy. "Here's your 'Christmas present,'" she said. "Somebody's got a sense of humor, that's for sure."

She watched Audy read the words on the page. "A *poem*?" she said with disbelief. "Somebody wrote a *poem* in code like this? What kind of joke is this?"

Stacy took the pad back and read. "Baby, it's cold outside... heart of winter in the city... the ice is slick, the circle thick... but, boy, it sure is pretty. Take 30 turns around the rink, then put your skates away... put on your shoes, pick up your bag... and begin a brand new day." Taking a sip of coffee, she said, "Not a very good poem. Pretty amateur. I wonder..." She looked over at Audy. "Are you OK? You look like you've seen a ghost."

Audy waved her hand, and took the pad back to read the words again. "I... this place... this sounds so familiar to me."

"The poem?"

Audy shook her head. "No," she said, "the place spoken of in the poem. It reminds me of..." Suddenly, she gasped, then reached into her purse, pulling out a small key. "Oh my God," she whispered as she rolled the key in her hand. "Now I know where I've seen this before! The rink! The skating rink! That's what he's talking about! That's where it's hidden!"

"Wha..." Stacy watched as Audy jumped from the booth, pulled on her coat and jammed the iPad in her purse. She grabbed the order pad, ripped off the sheet of paper with the poem, and shoved that into her purse as well. Without another word, Audy wrestled open the door, flew out of the restaurant and jumped into an old, dark sedan parked at the curb. With a screech of tires, the car pulled out into the night. Audy was gone.

And she hadn't left Stacy the promised tip. In fact, she hadn't even paid for her coffee.

Stacy sighed, got out of the booth, and bent to clear the table. So she didn't see the dark black SUV pull out behind Audy's car.

•••

Now, like I said, I am not a stupid woman. But sometimes I sure can act like one. Running off half-cocked when I understood the meaning of that poem was not one of my smarter moves. But I was so flabbergasted, so excited, so *convinced* that I knew exactly what I was doing, that I didn't stop to think.

I didn't stop to think who might be watching.

I was also pissed off in spades. My glorious, furious righteous indignation fueled my need for resolution to this god-awful mess. That's when I made a *really* stupid mistake. The mistake that would ultimately cost me my life. But, in my defense, I had no idea what I was about to discover.

Knowing it was close to midnight, I drove as fast as I could back to the apartment, careful not to plow down all the weaving revelers out celebrating the new year. I pulled into the loading dock, called Enrico, who hustled out and opened the door for me. He took one look at my face and knew something was up.

"Are you OK, Ms. Audrey?" he said with concern shining in his eyes. His eyes shot past me and out into the dark streets. "Did someone follow you? Did those stupido reporters come after you?"

"No, no, Enrico, I'm fine." I patted his shoulder as I shook my head. "I was just starting to run late, and I wanted to make sure I got your car back in time." I smiled at his concern. "Really, I'm fine. It's almost quitting time for you. Time to head home and celebrate the new year with your family."

Enrico looked at me, assessing. "No," he said in a firm voice, "you are not fine. You are up to something. I can tell. You have a spark in your eyes that I have not seen since they took Mr. Wade away. What is it? I cannot allow you to put yourself at risk. Mr. Wade is in serious trouble, and there are vicious men involved with him. If you know something, or have found out something, you must tell me so I can help you."

I looked at Enrico. His wide frame was taut with concern. His brown eyes looked directly into mine. Wade never looked into my eyes. He always was looking past me. The federal agents that had barged into my life were always looking for deception or clues. They never cared what I felt. But Enrico looked straight at me. His concern was evident. My heart said I could trust him. So I would.

"OK, Enrico," I said and took a deep breath. "I need a ride. I've got to pick something up."

"I'll take you. Of course," he said. "Let me check out and make sure Tony has come to work, and is sober." He shook his head. "Young lout," he said

117

about the night shift doorman, but he smiled. His look turned stern. "You stay right here," he warned.

He was back in two minutes, and climbed into the driver's side of the car. I slid over to the passenger seat.

"OK, where to?" he said as he started the engine again.

I looked out into the night. "The Ice Palace Skating rink," I said. "Off the LIE." I looked over at his puzzled expression. "Pull out and turn left. I'll tell you where to go."

A few dozen couples and families were turning slow circles around the outdoor skating rink as the lights highlighted soft, glittering snowflakes sifting down. Fireworks burst into color in the dark sky and Auld Lang Syne played over the loud speakers. I stopped for a moment, lost in memory. I used to come here as a kid, then a teen, when I could scrape together enough money. I'd skate for hours, trying to put distance between myself and the life I had waiting at home. I hadn't thought of this place in years. I hadn't even known it was still here. Wade and I had never been here together. Perhaps I had mentioned it to him, but I didn't think so. We rarely talked about my life *before.* He wasn't interested. And neither was I.

I scurried inside the clubhouse, where it was marginally warmer. Taking out the key, I moved along the banks of lockers, until I found the right number. Number 30. Just like in the poem. How many times had I used one of these to store my street shoes and bookbag?

The key fit easily into the lock and, after a few jiggles, the locker opened. I had to stop and force myself to take a deep breath. My breath had stopped up in my chest. With stern words to myself, I tried to keep a calm demeanor as I opened the locker. I didn't want to attract any attention.

That lasted until I opened the locker. Inside, on the bottom, was an old skating bag. *My* old skating bag. The one I kept down in the storage unit in our building. I pulled it out and held it for a moment, then slid the rusty zipper aside. Pulling it open just a little bit, I felt all the air leave my body and the blood flow down to my toes. I felt myself starting to fall to the floor, then quickly staggered to a bench and sat down. I pinched myself as hard as I could until I was sure I wasn't going to keel over. That would have been a disaster.

Because inside the bag was more money than I had ever seen before, even on television. And on top of the money was a big, shiny, loaded gun.

"A skate bag? That's what you had me drive all this way in the middle of the night to get?" Enrico was incredulous when I got back to the car and shoved the bag in the back seat, then hurriedly climbed into the passenger seat, locking the doors around us. I was seriously freaked out now, and just wanted to get home so I could figure out what to do.

I turned to Enrico. "Yes, a skate bag. Wade had made up a little game for me to play, a 'walk down memory lane,' as a holiday gift." I looked out at the rink again, trying to calm myself. "I used to come here as a kid. It was a nice time for me then, and I really wanted to get out here tonight. You know, with all that's been going on, I wanted to have a kind thought or two about Wade." I looked at Enrico out of the corner of my eye, to see if he believed me or not. He was skeptical, I knew, but he accepted my story.

Enrico started the car and we cruised out of the parking lot. Everyone was still out skating their way into the new year, except for one guy, a dark shadow in a dark SUV, who seemed to be sleeping in the driver's seat, waiting, perhaps, for his kids to finish skating. I watched him in the rear view mirror until we turned out of the parking lot, but he never moved. It wasn't until we were speeding along the Long Island Expressway that I allowed myself to relax a little.

We cruised around the building, and when Enrico was sure there were no reporters waiting for me, pulled around to the back of the loading dock and let me out.

"Well, this was an adventure, that's for certain," he said with a cheeky grin as he leaned out the window. "I'm not sure what *kind* of an adventure, but an adventure nonetheless. I can safely say that I have never had a New Year's Eve like this one, Ms. Audrey."

I laughed, short and sharp. "Me neither, Enrico. Me neither." I opened the back door and pulled out the skate bag with the money and the gun inside. It was heavy, both for body and soul. I had no idea what I had found, and I had no idea what I was going to do with it. I needed time to think. I had a sneaking suspicion that I was in *way* over my head, and I needed to dig up my old Bronx moxie so I could learn how to swim again and not get swallowed by the ferocious waves that were breaking over me from what I had found in that old locker.

I also did not want Enrico involved any further. He had done enough for me. I looked back into the eyes of my friend. You just never knew where you would meet a kindred spirit. In the lobby of your apartment building. Or in the old corner diner where you went to escape your present by burying yourself in the past you abhorred. I owed Enrico a lot.

I also owed Stacy the waitress some money.

It was way after midnight. I stood at the window in my living room, staring out at the bustling streets of Manhattan, listening to the sounds of horns and firecrackers and people laughing and calling to one another. Reflected in the glass, juxtaposed against the glittering skyline, was my living room sofa and coffee table. The couch was covered in piles and piles of money. The coffee table held the huge and menacing gun.

Happy New Year to me. I was in deep doo-doo. After counting it all twice, I discovered that the skating bag held over 20 million dollars, all wrapped in nice, tidy bundles. I still couldn't believe it. Even though the facts were staring me in the face, it was impossible for the information to sink into my frazzled brain. What had Wade done? What had I done?

The message on the iPad. Was that meant specifically for me? Was Wade expecting me to go and get the money for him if something happened to him? Or was it generic enough for any of his cronies to understand and follow? I didn't really know. But the thought of Wade involving me in his dirty dealings hurt. More than I expected. I felt like the poor slob on every cop TV show, the one who innocently steps into a huge pile of trouble just by getting out of bed on the morning in question. This whole fiasco was like something out of an episode of *Law and Order.* Special Victim's Unit.

That was me. The *Special Victim.* But this was too absurd to be fiction. This was my *life.* I had in my possession more money than I could have ever dreamed, even in my wild, get-out-of-the-Bronx-at-any-cost daydreams. I should have been dancing a jig, then bathing in champagne. But, instead, I was scared to death. I just wanted it all to go away.

I sat down in the middle of the piles of money and tried to put two thoughts together in my overloaded brain. Looking at my reflection in the huge picture window, I could not take it in. It was too ridiculous. I felt all my energy seeping out of my feet onto the plush carpet. I couldn't move if I'd tried.

Which is why I was just sitting there, staring into space, when I saw a dark, chiseled face with dark glasses appear behind my reflection in the window at the same time a strong, muscular arm wrapped around my throat and a large, long-fingered hand covered my mouth, cutting off my breath.

"Don't move," the voice said, deep and scratchy, whispering in my ear. "And don't try to scream." I immediately bit down on his hand, causing him to yank his hand away from my mouth, and let loose with a stream of cuss words that would make a sailor blush. I tried to pull away but he yanked me back on the couch and pressed his arm harder against my windpipe so I couldn't scream.

"I said 'Don't move!'" he said in a growl. "I'll snap your neck like a twig!" To prove his point, he pressed up and tight and I felt my head separating from my neck. I sank back into the couch and became perfectly still. Struggling would get me killed.

He moved and I felt the cold barrel of a gun press against the side of my neck. I looked at the coffee table and saw that the gun from the skating bag was still there. This guy carried his own weaponry. I closed my eyes as he said, "You are too stupid to live. Look at all this! Do you even realize what you've done?"

I stared at my pale, terrified face reflected next to his furiously angry one in the window and, amazingly, I nodded. For the first time, I really *did* know what I'd done. This guy looked like the same one that was sleeping the parking lot of the skating rink when Enrico and I had slunk by. He had followed me. Something else clicked and I realized that I had seen him before in the diner. When I'd been talking to Stacy the waitress about the number riddle. I'd been waving the iPad around like a flag, and this guy had been sitting watching me the whole time! God, I *was* too stupid to live! He had been following me for days. Here I was, sitting in a pile of money- stolen blood money- and one of Wade's "associates" had followed me, watched me "steal" his money, then broken into my house, to watch me count it out and then sit like the Queen of Everything right in the middle of it.

I couldn't breathe. I was so scared. So overwhelmed. So tired.

Suddenly, I gave up. I just gave up. My body became limp and the man beside me tightened his grip against the sudden extra weight as if to hold me up. He looked into my eyes in our reflection, then slowly loosened his grip around my neck. He took his hand off my mouth, leaving it hovering inches from my lips, in case I chose to start screaming. But I was beyond that.

"Just do it," I said wearily. "Just shoot me, get it over with. I don't care anymore. Just shoot me, get the money and go. Go bring it to Wade, or whoever your boss is. It's over. You guys win. It's all yours."

The guy in black looked at me incredulously. First his jaw sagged, then he snatched the dark glasses off and tossed them onto the coffee table. He came around the edge of the couch to stand in front of me, forcing me to look him in the eye. He held the gun in front of him, aimed at my chest. I looked past the gun, to his face. He was really, really angry.

"Is that what you think?" he asked in a deep, harsh voice. "Is that who you think I am? Some kind of mob goon? One of your husband's lackeys? Boy, lady, you really are stupid! You just have no idea!" He shook his head, ran his hand down the back of his neck, rubbing hard. Looking down, he realized the gun was still in his hand, pointed at me. He let out an exasperated sigh, then turned and tossed the gun onto the coffee table. It landed with a thud and slid up next to the gun already sitting there.

He turned back to me. "Lady," he said as if he were talking to a five-year-old, "I'm not the guy you should be worried about." He shoved his hands in his pockets. "Oh, you should be plenty worried. The goons are out there, waiting on every corner. Waiting for you to leave this apartment, so that they can come in and find that iPad with the message on it." He shook his head again. "They just weren't paying close enough attention. They didn't expect you to have the gumption to actually do the job yourself. They were looking for you to leave by the front door in your fancy coat with your fancy heels. They never expected you to sneak out the service elevator."

He looked at her, drawing his brows together in a puzzled frown. "They underestimated you." He tilted his head to one side. "Just like you underestimated me." He reached into his back pocket and pulled out a leather wallet. He flipped it open and held it out to her so she could see it. Another big, shiny badge. She looked up at him.

"Special Agent Christopher Mancuso," he said. "FBI. Undercover Racketeering and Organized Crime Detail." He paused. "And protector of crazy old ladies."

I looked at this guy, looked at the guns sitting on the table. OK, so perhaps he was one of the good ones. But the bad guys were waiting just outside my door. They were hard to tell apart on the outside.

I stared at him and thought a little closer to home. To my own life. Who are the bad guys in my own house? Who are the heroes? I couldn't really answer that question. It was hard to tell the difference. Both Wade and I had made our mistakes. The lines had become blurred. Wade was guilty, there was no doubt. All I had to do was look at the predicament I was in- money scattered everywhere, a gun gleaming on my coffee table like some sort of perverted centerpiece, the man in black taking up too much space in my living room.

But wasn't I also guilty? In many ways, I had done exactly as Wade had, albeit without the bloodshed, the mob connections and the looming jail sentence. I had longed for money, for escape, for the false gold and the glittery edges that would smooth away the roughness of my upbringing and make me into something I certainly was not. Marrying Wade and his money hadn't given me anything. And now I was sitting in money up to my eyeballs. And it wasn't bringing me one iota of comfort. I had allowed my own lines to become blurred. I didn't know which I was- a good guy or a bad one.

But I knew which I *wanted* to be.

Chris Mancuso was looking at me with those deep, blue eyes that told nothing. I found I was no longer scared of him. I found I was no longer scared of my situation. I felt a growing strength inside me. My old Bronx moxie was finally rising to the surface. I was tired of being scared. I was tired of trying to fix everybody else's problems. I was tired of living this big, fat, ridiculous lie.

I looked over at Chris Mancuso, who narrowed his eyes and leaned forward in his chair. "Wow," he said. "I can actually see the wheels turning in your head." He tilted his head to one side. "What exactly is going on in that sleek little mind of yours?"

I picked up thick pile of cash and held it, fanning out the bills with my index finger. Then I calmly set it aside and reached over and picked up Chris Mancuso's gun from the coffee table. I held it out to him and he slowly reached out to take it from me. I then picked up the gun I'd found in the skating bag and held it in both hands. It was cold. And heavy. Good guys and bad guys. Heroes and villains. New Year's Eve. Resolutions. I looked at my reflection in the big plate glass window of my gilded living room. Can someone make a New Year's resolution to become a completely different person? Can someone make a resolution to stop covering their real selves up with a weak alter-ego and become a super hero?

I took a deep breath and squared my shoulders. A plan clicked into place. One that would end this charade once and for all. I resolved to be a hero, even if only in my own life. Not everyone would know. But the important people would. I would. And that's all that mattered.

I turned the gun over and over in my hands and looked up at Chris Mancuso. "I am sick of all this," I said calmly. "Sick of the money. Sick of the lies. Sick of the unpleasant surprises that seem to wait on every corner. And sick of the cloak and dagger crap that you big boys seem to enjoy playing." I narrowed my own eyes as he leaned back, ready to defend his job. "Oh, I know you think you're doing a good deed." I held up my hand as he drew in a breath. "And maybe you are. But it's not doing any good. One day it's your side. The next day it's theirs. When is it going to stop?"

I shook my head and looked back down at the gun. "I am sick to death of all this. I looked up into Chris' face. "Sick to death of who I am and how I live. Sick of being a criminal just because I married one. It's time for me to do something about that. I just want to be free of it all." I looked at him without blinking. "I think the only way to be free is to be dead."

I chuckled when I saw the look on Chris' face. He was a good guy after all, I thought. Nice to know.

I explained my plan. He listened carefully. Getting up from his chair, he walked over to look out the window. He looked out for a long time. Then he turned to me. "OK," he said with a sigh, then pursed his lips and straightened his shoulders. "OK." He pointed at the gun in my hand. He smiled a crooked smile. "Want me to show you how to use that thing?"

•••

Chris Mancuso carefully laid the newspaper down alongside his coffee cup and turned to look out the window. The old broad had managed to pull it off. He looked down at the front page headline again and shook his head. "Socialite Commits Suicide" the headline shouted. Underneath, in smaller print, the tag line read, "Audrey Walters kills self in wake of husband's arrest surrounded by embezzled funds."

He had helped set it up, after getting permission from the FBI chairman. It required some serious finesse, especially with the Walter's woman's "requirements." Extra cash was brought in. Audrey posed like a silent-movie actress, spread out across the big brocade couch, the gun next to her limp hand, cash spread all around her. Tasteful, yet effective, she'd said. An FBI photographer got the "exclusive" photos of the scene, which was then sent off to all the major news outlets. A body bag was rolled out in full view of the media frenzy in front of her building. Then, bags of cash, carried out by big, burly FBI agents, were hauled out to waiting SUV's with darkened windows. It was enough evidence to haul in the rest of Wade Walter's "associates" and convince any jury that the scumbags should be put away for life. All the money was accounted for. Just not all of it made it to the courthouse.

Chris saw Stacy the waitress come around the corner, heading for her shift at the diner. She held a folded newspaper under her arm and, by the look on her face, she had read the day's headlines. She pulled open the door, letting in a gust of cold wind, then headed for the counter area. She hung up her coat, put on an apron and put the newspaper in a cubby under the counter.

Chris saw her frown, then pull out a bag from the cubby. She pulled out an envelope. She turned the envelope around and Chris could see her name scrawled on the front. Gingerly, she opened the envelope and gasped. At the same time her cell phone jingled an incoming text message. Looking around to make sure no one was looking over her shoulder, she closed the envelope and pulled her phone from her apron pocket. She looked down at the screen, frowned, and maneuvered around the screen. She looked again, then lifted the newspaper, scanning the front page, looking for information.

Setting the newspaper down, she picked up the phone again and punched in a number. Her head jerked up when his phone began signaling an incoming call. Scanning the room, her eyes locked on his.

"Hello?" he said, answering the call. His eyes never strayed from hers.

"We need to talk," she said, her eyes boring straight through to his soul.

"Yes, we do," he said, and ended the call.

•••

It is a very weird thing to read about your own death in the newspaper. Doing it while sitting in a hammock sipping a mai tai helps, I have to admit. But it's still weird.

When I decided to become a hero, my first order of business was to take my life back. That may sound odd since the front page of the paper shows a photo of me laying in a dramatic death pose with a gun lying on the floor next to me, dropped by my lifeless hand while surrounded by piles and piles of money. But I knew for sure that the only way I would be able to live is if everyone else thought I was dead.

Once Chris Mancuso got past the point where he thought I'd lost the few marbles I had left, he really got into the spirit of the thing. I'm not sure if his main motivation was to save my life from the thugs lining up to get me, or at the thought of making a watertight case against my husband and "associates." Probably a little bit of both. Whatever the case, he crossed the "t's" and dotted the "i's" of my absurd plan, guaranteeing a fool-proof getaway for me and a life prison term for Wade and his friends.

Everything was going fine until I brought up the fact that I was not going to leave this life empty handed. I had *earned* part of that money and I was taking some of it with me. Enough to live on for the rest of my life. And enough to pay off a couple of debts. For every excuse he had I stood my ground and

wouldn't budge. I stood toe to toe with Chris Mancuso and every member of the FBI he brought with him. Turns out you can take the girl out of the Bronx, but you can never take the Bronx out of the girl.
I was still one tough babe. With a decent manicure.

That's the "hero" part.

So, we set it up. A fake suicide. Enough fake money to make it seem like it was all there, even though a few mil was in my suitcase. Enough evidence to buy Wade a one-way ticket to Riker's. And the piece de resistance- a tear-stained, melodramatic note that would convince even the most hardened criminal that I had gone to that great big gala in the sky. Chris played his role to the hilt, speaking solemnly to the news media, giving just enough information to make it all sound accurate, never lying outright. At just the right moment, he "leaked" the suicide note to the press.

Then he drove me to the airport. But not before we made a couple of small stops. He pulled up to the small plane waiting for me and handed off my suitcase filled with a few clothes and a lot of cash. We stood in the dark, wondering what to say to each other. In some sort of weird way, we'd become friends.

I reached out and gave him a quick kiss, then reached up and patted his cheek. "Have a nice life," I said.

He grabbed my hand, squeezed it in both of his, then let go. He stuck his hands in his pockets, rocked back on his heels and gave me that little half smile of his.

"Have a nice death," he said.

"I will," I promised him and, clutching my suitcase, turned and crawled into the plane. And I meant it.

I celebrate all my holidays now among a new family... a family that looks remarkably like my friend, Enrico. He and his wife and son will be here day after tomorrow to celebrate the holiday. He's got plenty of time now. He doesn't have to worry about money much anymore. The packet of unmarked bills he found under the front seat of his car will keep him comfortable for the rest of his days. So he comes back to this small town in a country south of the border often to see his family . And me. His travel route is different each time. Always, he is thinking about my safety. He'll never tell. And neither will I.

Last time he visited, he brought a copy of the *Times*. He handed it to me with a grin, said "page 3" and then went off to greet the relatives.

I turned to the correct page and smiled. There, smiling back at me, was Stacy, the waitress from the diner. She was dressed in a lovely designer suit in front of a building that said, "Food for Thought." It looked suspiciously like the old diner. The caption read: "Dining with a purpose. Local woman creates a menu for education. " Stacy the waitress had taken her "windfall" and created a place where people could go and get continuing education, mentoring and work experience. A way up or a way out of the projects.

Not only had Stacy gotten the life she wanted, but she made it so she was giving others a chance as well. In the neighborhood she had fought so hard to get out of. It had turned out that, in her case, you can take the Bronx out of the girl, but you couldn't get the girl to leave the Bronx.

I looked at the photo again. Peered closer. My smile grew. There, in the background was Chris Mancuso. Still wearing the same black leather jacket. But he wasn't scowling. His dark eyes were fixed on Stacy. And he was grinning from ear to ear.

As for resolutions, well, I don't make them anymore. I made the changes I needed to make. I am where I belong. I do the things that I know are right. I think I served justice in some small way. Most of all, I have come to find out that money really doesn't change anything. It's worthless without love. I had worked hard to get out of the Bronx and become a person I didn't know, and certainly didn't like. And I had married a stranger, a man I shared my most intimate moments with, but never really knew. Together, and separately, we had strove only for money, and the comfort it was supposed to bring. In the end, we had both paid a price.

Resolutions are a chance to take a good look at yourself, see what works, see what doesn't. It's an opportunity to take control of your life *from this moment on.* No looking back. No blaming anybody else. You can't do anything about the past. But you can do something about the future. You can become the hero of your own life… and maybe someone else's.

I am a girl from the Bronx made good. Who knew?

I spend a bit of time each year writing a short holiday story that I include in our Christmas letter to family and friends. Last year, though, I had the hardest time finishing the story I was working on and getting it out to print. I worked and worked on it, but the right words never seemed to come. Something was holding me back.

Then, the first week of December, there was a mass shooting in a mall where my family often goes. Within forty-eight hours of that, the horrible shooting at Sandy Hook Elementary School occurred.

These words flowed from me in less than fifteen minutes.

My Christmas Wish for You

For the victims of violence everywhere-

Season's Greetings, 2012

As usual, I had a nice, happy holiday story all written to send out. And maybe I'll still send it later. But it has not been a "usual" week. This year's holiday "story" is still being written. Reality this year is not silver and gold, or wrapped in pretty paper tied in a bright bow.

We live near Clackamas Town Center, the scene of a mass shooting last week. It's the mall where we usually go, and, but for the grace of God, it's entirely possible that we could have been there that day, ordering late lunch in the food court or picking up a gift at Macy's. Life can change in an instant. And we don't even know it's coming.

Increasingly over the years, city after city, town after town lays claim to the dark legacy of that moment of insanity that cuts futures short and leaves families devastated. There is a line drawn that separates **then** from **now**. I'm sure that there is a person in Newtown, Connecticut, or in Aurora, Colorado, or in Chicago, or Littleton, or New York that wishes right this minute that they could turn the clock back to **then** and have one last *regula*r day. Nothing spectacular. Just a day where everything is as it should be...and everyone is home for dinner.

It's Christmas. A time for giving and receiving. Of hoping. Of wishing. I know what I want for Christmas. And I wish the same for you.

- I wish for you a day when you stand waiting in line at the grocery store long enough to have read the current issue of every tabloid cover, but have enough in the checking account to pay for what you bought.

- I wish for you a faucet that drips, a floor that creaks, a wall that needs painting. A place to put your feet up. A place that's warm and dry. *Home.*
- I wish for you work that fills your days and pays your bills.
- I wish for you a body that may groan a bit but still gets you where you want to go.
- I wish for you a day of Facebook friends, text messages, Pinterest, and email jokes.
- I wish for you a day at the mall, complaining about prices, looking for a bargain. Then I wish for you the ability to get in your car and leave- a little overheated, legs a little stiff, with a half-finished Orange Julius clutched in your hand. Safe and sound.
- I wish for you a day where the unexpected shrill of the phone is just a friend you haven't heard from in a while. A day, like every other day, when the door bangs open, exactly on time, a backpack drops with a thud that makes you wince and a young voice bellows, "I'm home!"
- I wish for you a trip to the theater for a movie with too much popcorn and a happy ending.

- I wish for you one of <u>those </u>days. A regular day. Where the "stuff" of your life makes you a bit crazy, leaves you a tad bored, or craving an extra hour or two. A day of errands, car pools and soccer practice. And a long evening of sitcoms or ballgames with everyone you love sprawled around the family room. A day you can count on. One where you know what's coming... and no one changes it.
- Most of all, I wish for you a string of those days that melt into months, moving with the seasons, through the year. And for all of us, whether I have met you or not- I wish you PEACE.

www.ingramcontent.com/pod-product-compliance
Lightning Source LLC
Chambersburg PA
CBHW060621130626
46555CB00002B/599